D1648100

DEFENDING HOME

THE LONG ROAD HOME
BOOK 10

CAITLYN O'LEARY

© Copyright 2022 Caitlyn O'Leary
All rights reserved.
All cover art and logo © Copyright 2022
By Passionately Kind Publishing Inc.
Cover by Cat Johnson
Edited by Rebecca Hodgkins
Content Edited by Trenda Lundin
Photograph by Rob Lang
ISBN: 978-1-949849-51-6

If you find any eBooks being sold or shared illegally, please contact the author at Caitlyn@CaitlynOLeary.com.

To everyone who puts up with me as I work down to the wire. My husband John, Drue Hoffman, Trenda London, and Rebecca Hodgkins. I couldn't do this without your support.

Will Two Tormented Souls Have The Courage To Reach For Love?

The only family Nolan O'Rourke ever claimed were his Navy SEAL brothers; they had never let him down. His childhood wasn't rough, it wasn't hard, it was hell, and now any mission that he was assigned to was a cakewalk in comparison.

When Nolan finds out that his mother, the woman who made his childhood a nightmare, died giving birth to his baby sister, it was decision time. Could he handle going back to Tennessee, even though he'd sworn never to step foot in Jasper Creek ever again?

Mary Smith is in trouble. Twenty-eight months, three states, and three names ago she was still on the run from a man intent on killing her. Now she finds herself in a trailer park in the middle of nowhere Tennessee, ready to run again at the slightest provocation. But she has a problem; a tiny bundle wrapped in a pink blanket. How could she have promised a dead woman that she'd take care of her baby?

Will two people who don't believe in trust or love, come together to save a life, and possibly make their own lives worth living?

PROLOGUE

Nolan couldn't duck in time—the fist hit his jaw and he went down. Willie, Arlo, and Titus stood over him and laughed. The dirt from the playground mixed with the blood from his split lip. He stood up fast before Titus got in a kick, which was what usually happened. Willie hit, Arlo laughed, and Titus kicked.

"You gonna run away and tell teacher?" Willie taunted.

"Iffin you do, we'll tell Mizz Blanchette you started it," Arlo sneered. "Titus's daddy owns the bank, everybody believes anything he says, and you're just trailer trash."

Nolan knew better than to ask why they beat on him, he'd done that in first and second grade. The answer was always some version of, "*Your mama is a whore, and you shouldn't be allowed in school with regular kids. You should just go back to your trailer, where you belong.*"

One day he'd be a big kid. He'd be the biggest kid, and he'd show them!

"Aren't you going to say something? Or are you too chicken?" Titus wanted to know.

"Look at him, Willie, he's going to wet his pants. Remember when he did that?" Arlo jeered.

Nolan flushed because that *had* happened in first grade. That day he didn't take the bus home, he'd left school from the playground and tried to find his way back to the trailer park by himself. He got lost for a long time. Finally, the postman took him in his truck to his house. He was nice.

Now he stood before the three boys, his arms down at his sides, his fists clenched.

"Look at the little baby, he thinks he can fight us." Willie pointed to his fists. "Is that what you want Noooo-Good? Do you want to fight me?"

He hated that name. Now all the kids called him No-Good instead of Nolan.

"Answer me. You gonna fight us?" Willie demanded to know.

Reluctantly, Nolan shook his head. Even though he hated Willie and hated that nickname, he knew he would just end up more bruised and bloody, and it would make it tougher to help his mom go to the store for food when he got home.

"No-Good O'Rourke is a scaredy-cat," Arlo laughed. "Y'all, what's the point of beating on him, if he won't even fight back?"

Willie ran two steps forward and punched Nolan

in the gut. He ended up on the ground again, this time he hurt a lot worse.

"I'll tell you why you beat on him. Because if we leave him still standing, he hasn't learned his lesson. He doesn't belong with good folks, ain't that right, Titus?"

Nolan was holding his stomach, writhing on the ground in the fetal position. Willie was the biggest boy in class, and his hits hurt.

"My daddy says that No-Good and his Ma need to leave town. He says they're a disgrace to every good person in this town." Nolan heard the smile in Titus's voice. He needed to get up before he was kicked.

"I should help make them leave, that would sure make my daddy happy."

"No, not in the head, you'll get in real trouble, Titus," Willie protested. "Kick him in the back."

"Yeah," Arlo agreed.

Nolan tried to roll into the smallest ball possible so that Titus would have a tiny target, but when he kicked the toe of his cowboy boot into Nolan's lower back, it didn't matter—pain exploded and he cried out.

"You're going to be sharing your room with Michael. He just got here a couple of weeks ago, so he was really hoping we could bring a friend home for him to play with. We were so happy when they told us a little boy was coming to stay with us."

Yeah, sure.

Nolan looked around at the room he was supposed to stay in. It looked too big. Too clean.

This can't be right.

"Who's Michael? Where's he at?" he asked Mrs. Sherman.

"He's at school. It's the last week, so he's going to finish it out, but you're going to stay home with me. We talked to the doctors and everyone thought that would be best."

"What's the name of the school?" Nolan asked.

"Riverview. It was just built five years ago. It has a really nice playground and gymnasium; I think you'll like it. You're in the same grade as Michael, so you'll both have each other to play with this summer, *and* when you both go back to school."

Nolan quit looking at the woman's knees. He needed to see if she was a liar. A lot of adults were liars.

His mom was a liar.

Most of her friends were liars.

His teacher at the old school was a liar. She always said she would listen to his side of the story, but she never did.

Even the lady at the hospital was a liar. He said he wanted to go home, and she said if he told the truth about what it was like living with his mom, she'd 'valuate it and make sure he had the best home possible. She was a tricker, which was worse than a liar. Now who was going to make sure his mom used some of her money for food?

Nolan wasn't dumb, he knew his mom's friends

liked mom to give them money for all that goop that made her act stupid, tired, and sometimes angry, sometimes crazy, and sometimes really, really nice and happy. But when she paid them, then they didn't have food. His mom needed food even more than he did... well, sometimes. A lot of times he was awful hungry.

Nolan had explained that to the lady. He explained that he had to take care of his mom, and it was important he leave the hospital and go back to her. She said she would 'valuate it. And now the tricker had taken Nolan on a long car ride to Mrs. Sherman's house and he was supposed to share a room with a strange kid named Michael. How was he supposed to get back home to fix things for his mom?

"Thank you for looking at me, Nolan, you sure are a handsome boy."

Why'd she say that? Mom always says I'm ugly.

"Why don't you set your things there on the bed. The blanket with race cars on it is yours."

Nolan turned around and saw that the other bed had dinosaurs, but the one she'd pointed to had race cars. But it might be a trick.

"It's only for the first day, right?"

She looked confused. "What do you mean the first day, Nolan?"

"The blanket. It's special. Where's my real blanket?"

Nolan looked around the room for some kind of blanket tossed in a corner. That would be his.

Mrs. Sherman knelt down in front of him and

touched his hand like she wanted to hold it, but he jerked it away. For just a second she frowned and he knew he was in for it, but then she smiled again.

"Nolan, that comforter with the race cars is always going to be yours, no matter what. I won't let anyone take it away from you. I promise."

She looked nice. Her eyes were funny colored. They were green and brown and gray, but nice. Maybe she wasn't tricking him.

"Do you want to take out your belongings and get them put away?" she asked.

"Under the bed?"

She smiled again and stood up. She walked a few steps and put her hand on a blue dresser. "The three drawers on this side belong to you. You can put your things in here."

"Okay."

He sure had lucked out. If he really got to keep the blanket, then it was loads better than dinosaurs! Nolan carefully put his black garbage sack on the bed and started to pull out his stuff. He didn't know what was in it, the tricker lady at the hospital had said she would get his things from his trailer, not him. Something about it not being safe in his house, and there being needles. It didn't make any sense. There were always needles, you just had to be careful not to step on 'em. She was dumb and a tricker.

He pulled out some jeans and underwear and stuff, but when his hand hit the pointy plastic, his breath caught.

Really?

No way.

He carefully pulled it out of the bottom of the sack. He had to be careful because it was already broken, so he didn't want it to break even more. When he saw the red mask his breath caught again and he almost wanted to cry, but he didn't.

It was his Lego Vakama that he'd found near the trailer park dumpster after Christmas. It was his very own Bionicle. Sure, his one arm and disk launcher were missing, but who cared? Vakama was the very best of the Bionicles!

Nolan examined him carefully. He made sure that the one remaining arm could still move. When he moved the gear on the back, it could!

"What's that?" Mrs. Sherman asked in a soft voice.

Nolan had forgotten she was even there. He hugged Vakama to his chest.

"Nothing."

Mrs. Sherman smiled. "Nolan, under your bed is your very own box, and it's only for you. No one else in the house can go into it without your permission. So, if you want to put your toy in there at night, or when you have to leave for school or day camp, you can put him in there."

Nolan bent down and looked under the bed. There was a red box. He walked over to Michael's bed and found a green box.

"So, he has his own, and he won't need to come into mine?"

"That's right," Mrs. Sherman tried to assure him.

"Okay." But Nolan didn't let go of Vakama. No way. No how.

"Nolan, I bet you're hungry. Would you like to have a sandwich and then chocolate cake for dessert?"

Was she foolin'? He'd test her again.

"Now? You have the food here?"

Mrs. Sherman stopped smiling, but she nodded. "Yes, Honey, I have the food here. I have it in my kitchen. I can either make you a peanut butter and jelly sandwich or a grilled cheese sandwich. Which would you like me to make for you?"

Nolan still wasn't convinced.

"You have the bread here?"

Mrs. Sherman sighed and knelt down in front of him. "I do have everything I told you. I can even give you a glass of milk or apple juice. Why don't you come into the kitchen and see for yourself?"

Nolan thought about it. "Yeah. Let me see."

Mrs. Sherman held out her hand for him to hold, but he couldn't do it.

She sighed, but still kept smiling at him.

"If you like chocolate cake, maybe I'll make brownies tomorrow."

I hope she isn't a tricker.

CHAPTER ONE

Navy SEAL, Nolan O'Rourke looked down at the last letter he'd received from Ginger Rose Hannity O'Rourke, otherwise known as his mother. The letter had come while he was out on one of the longest missions of his life. Not so long ago, he'd pulled out a black Sharpie, and wrote 'RETURN TO SENDER', and had felt a sense of relief flow through him.

It hadn't lasted long.

He shoved Ginger's letter into the pocket of his leather jacket and then pulled out the other letter. The one that he *had* opened from a woman named Mary Smith. Maybe he would've been smarter to open the one from Ginger O'Rourke instead.

God help me!

Nolan began reading Mary's letter again, even though he now knew every line by heart.

. . .

Dear Mr. O'Rourke,

You don't know me, but I was a friend of your mother. My name is Mary Smith, and for the past year before Ginger died, Ginger and I became good friends. I'm reaching out to you because I don't know what else to do. A little over three months ago, your mother died giving birth to a baby girl. She is the most precious baby imaginable. Ginger made me the baby's guardian, but I'm going to need to leave soon.

Your mother's things were lost for a while, so it wasn't until yesterday that I was able to read the letters that Ginger wrote to you, and that you had sent back unopened. If you had opened them you would know that she loved you very much and is so sorry for how she treated you when you were a child and all those other times when you were a teenager. I know she wanted to make amends. I hope you will have it in your heart to come and take care of your sister before she ends up in the foster system like you did.

Sincerely
    Mary Smith
    Jasper Creek, TN

Mary had left her phone number and address. The only person that Nolan had shown this letter to was

Gideon Smith. Gideon was second in command of his SEAL team and was without a doubt the smartest man he knew when it came to computers and unearthing information. Nolan had hated to bring Gideon into his personal business. He hated talking about his past.

Which is why I never do.

Full stop!

Only this time, he didn't have a choice. He'd tried to find out things about Ginger Rose Hannity O'Rourke and only found an obituary notice. It said she was survived by her only daughter, Iris Rose Hannity. What fucked up shit was that? For God's sake, it was fine that he wasn't mentioned—as a matter of fact, it was better. But why did Iris have his mother's maiden name, and not the father's?

The whole thing was fishy as hell. Was it possible that Mary Smith had given birth to the baby girl, and was now trying to get him to take care of her while she took off to parts unknown? After all, Ginger had to be at least forty-two or forty-three years old. Wasn't she too old to have another kid?

Those were the questions that had nagged him for the first eight hours after having received the letter. Then after finding out some vague answers, it led him here, touching down at the Atlanta airport, ready to take a connecting flight to Knoxville, where he'd then drive to the town of his birth—Jasper Creek, Tennessee.

Nolan didn't know whether to feel irritated or relieved that his flight to Knoxville had been delayed. He shifted his pack and considered getting one of the sad-looking ham and cheese sandwiches in the kiosk since he knew he had to wait at minimum another seven hours. He picked it up and saw that the lettuce looked more brown than green.

Nope. I don't want to tempt fate.

"I want candy," a small child whined softly.

"You can't have any more candy," a tired mother denied.

"You promised to read me a story," another child complained bitterly.

"He's hitting me," yet another child's voice yelled petulantly.

"Aaaaaahhhhh." The wail of a baby.

It was almost as bad as being in combat, the way the cacophony of sounds pelted him all at once. Nolan turned around and saw a young woman who looked near tears. She was crouching down while holding the baby who was screaming like a banshee, and the three other kids were coming at her from all angles.

Nolan listened for two more minutes, and when he saw the mother go down on one knee and start pleading with the littlest girl, he figured it couldn't get any worse if he stepped in.

"Okay, whichever one of you can name the airport we're in, you'll win a quarter. Is it a deal?"

All three blondes looked up at him with big brown eyes. They nodded.

The mother gave him a relieved look and mouthed, 'Thank you' then moved up a spot in the line.

"Part of the deal is, you've gotta step out of line, let your mom buy her stuff, and stand where she can see you. Can you do that?"

"Show me the quarter," the oldest little girl said with a scowl.

Nolan laughed. He couldn't help it. She couldn't be more than six years old, but even at her age, she wasn't going to be taken advantage of. He fished around in his jeans pocket and came up with a quarter. "Satisfied?"

All three of them nodded. Out of the corner of his eye, he saw their mom putting some aspirin and antihistamine on the counter. Now that she didn't have the rest of her tribe to worry about, she seemed to have been able to soothe her baby.

"I want the quarter," the youngest girl said.

"You have to earn it," Nolan told her. "Now which one of you can tell me which airport we're in?"

He watched the two girls and the little boy think about it. They were so damn little. He couldn't imagine ever having been that small. The boy's face lit up.

"The big airport!"

"No, that's a stupid name," his older sister chastised him. Nolan watched as her head swiveled around, taking in her environment. "It's the passenger airport," she said.

The smallest girl took her thumb out of her mouth. "Atlanta. Daddy left us here," her smile wobbled.

"He's coming back," the little boy patted his little sister's shoulder.

God, they were all cute. He wondered what his teammate Sebastian Durand, and his wife were going to have, another little boy or a girl this time?

Nolan knelt down. "You're right, Sweetheart. It's the Atlanta Airport."

She smiled at him and slapped her chest in glee. "Do I get a quarter?"

"Yes, you do." He handed it over to her.

"You really don't have to do that, sir."

Nolan looked up and saw that the woman was actually pretty when she wasn't so harassed.

"No, she earned the quarter fair and square." Nolan smiled at the mother.

"Well, thank you for entertaining them while I made that purchase." He saw she had the baby calmed down and in a stroller. "I'll be happy when my husband parks the car and makes it inside so we can get through security together, but he said to just go on ahead if he isn't here on time."

Seriously? What kind of douchenozzle would leave his wife alone to deal with all of this?

"It wasn't a problem, ma'am," Nolan assured her.

"Well, we better head to security. Say thank you to the nice man, Charlotte."

The little girl took her thumb out of her mouth again and gave him a sleepy smile, then mumbled a 'thank you'.

"Goodbye, and thank you again," the mother said.

"I had fun," Nolan said truthfully and gave her a half smile then waved to the small family as they headed toward the long security line.

What an asshole. What kind of man would leave his woman with four young kids to handle everything?

Nolan sighed and started toward the USO.

As soon as he stepped over the threshold into the USO, he was met with a bright smile.

"Hello," the elegant woman greeted him. Nolan was taken aback since he was still thinking about the poor woman having to struggle through security without her husband.

The woman tilted her head as she pushed the sign-in book toward him. "Something on your mind? You look troubled."

Nolan shook his head. "It's not anything I can fix." He looked down at the registration desk. "Is this where I sign in, ma'am?"

The smiling woman nodded.

Nolan set down his backpack and signed in. He told himself to shake off his crap mood and smile at the lady who was making such an effort.

"The name's Nolan O'Rourke," he offered.

"Well, it's good to make another friend." Her smile got even wider. "My name is Blessing, and I'm your tour guide this evening. You wouldn't be heading out on the flight to Knoxville, would you?"

Nolan gave her a surprised look. "How did you guess that?" he asked.

"There's a young man I still keep in touch with. He and his wife are both from Gatlinburg. There's music in their accent. You have it too."

Nolan stuffed down a laugh.

"Music, huh?"

"Absolutely. Well, let's get you situated. If you'd follow me?"

Nolan nodded. As he followed her down the hall, she pointed to a wall of shelves and cubbies. "You can put your backpack here. Don't worry, it's safe."

Nolan trusted her and shoved his pack into the nearest space available. As they passed another opening he saw men, women, and kids lounging about and sleeping. Some of the kids were as young as the ones he'd just encountered near the kiosk.

"Most of these people are families who have either missed their connecting flights or their flights have been canceled," she whispered. "The children have been very quiet and well behaved, so I don't expect them to be any kind of problem, but since you like children, I know you won't be annoyed."

Nolan stopped in his tracks.

"I beg your pardon, ma'am?" he whispered again. "What gave you the idea I liked children?"

Blessing looked up at him with a twinkle in her eye. "The tiny chocolate handprint on the front of your uniform. And it's a good thing too, considering what's coming up when you get home. Those two little ladies are lucky to have you fighting their corner."

Huh? She couldn't possibly know anything about what's going on, could she? Two?

Nolan shook his head like he was trying to get water out of his ear.

"I'm sorry, Mizz Blessing, but I'm not quite tracking with what you're saying."

"It's just that I suspect you've quite the row to hoe when you get home, but I know you'll get through it, dear." She patted his arm. "Now let me show you to where I've got you sitting."

"Okay." Nolan followed her with a frown on his face.

She went a little farther down the hall and he soon found himself in an empty room with really comfortable-looking leather seats.

How'd I rate?

Before he could ask the question, Blessing smiled at him.

"I like to put the right people together. Sometimes it's good when people who are going through transitions or struggles in their lives meet others going through the same thing."

Nolan took another look around the empty room.

"Okay," he said tentatively.

Blessing let out a big laugh. It was a pretty laugh. "Oh, Nolan, trust me, you won't be alone for long, and I really think you'll find others that you can rely on who'll truly understand what you're going through."

"I beg your pardon, ma'am, but—"

"Now you sit down and make yourself comfortable. I have to get back to my post."

Strange didn't even begin to cover that whole encounter, but the woman had figured out a lot about him with just a little bit of input. Did she know even more?

Nolan shook his head. He didn't have time to focus on Mizz Blessing, he had bigger fish to fry.

He sat down in one of the most comfortable chairs he'd ever sat in and closed his eyes for a moment. He stopped himself before pulling out Mary Smith's letter again. There would be time enough for obsessing on the flight to Knoxville. Right now, he just needed to relax, and rest up for whatever he'd find in Jasper Creek. God knew it was sure to be some kind of shitshow.

Chapter Two

Nolan scrubbed the back of his neck, trying to work out the kinks. Waiting for the rental car was going to take longer than the flight from Atlanta to Knoxville. At least he'd had a bit of a respite while he'd been at the USO when he'd met the other men. Good guys. Really good guys. How in the hell he'd managed to be stuck at the airport with three other SEALs was a mystery to him, and even though Dylan Grant was Army, he'd fit right in. Especially when he'd told them his story about the whoo-whoo shit that Blessing had 'blessed' him with.

All five of them were trying to figure out if the woman was a kook, a mystic, or a blessing. But the way they all were kind of reeling from what she'd had to say, had Nolan thinking mystic might be more the mark. They'd all exchanged numbers, which was also kind of weird because he was normally only close with his teammates, but again, the whole night seemed a little otherworldly.

Which is how he'd ended up with Scott Evers, Chris Andrews, Dylan Grant, and Cal Swenson's numbers all logged into his phone...and he'd even noted Blessing's last name so he could get in touch with her, in case...well, just in case.

Nolan looked at the harried faces of the rental car employees as they told even more unhappy customers that their cars were coming from Nashville and would be a while.

Nolan kept his happy ass planted in the plastic seat and pulled out his phone to see if his teammate, Landon Kelly had texted him again to tell him about the woman he was dating. He rolled his eyes. That boy fell in love faster and more often than a bunny. But there was nothing. After checking the sports scores, he closed his eyes and tried to will himself into a state of Zen, but it wasn't working. Instead, he kept thinking about everything that brought him to this moment.

After an ungodly mission in Eastern Europe that had

lasted forever and sapped the life out of his entire team, he'd come home to his apartment to find a letter from his mom that had been lost in the mail for almost six months. It was just the cherry on top of a turd sandwich, and he got out his Sharpie and wrote RETURN TO SENDER in big bold letters. Then he found another fucking letter from Jasper Creek and almost shredded that one along with all the coupon flyers and political junk mail.

He hated his hometown with a passion. The problem was, the letter was addressed to Chief Petty Officer Nolan O'Rourke, and it was written in a pretty script, and it captured his imagination. There wasn't a chance in hell that his mother could have written it; there was no way her handwriting could have changed that much and she'd never cared enough to figure out his rank.

Nolan turned the letter over and found that it was sealed with a freakin' butterfly sticker. Yep, definitely not his mom, but definitely a woman, or a girl for that matter. But no, the writing wasn't loopy like a girl's, and there was the fact that she knew his rank. It was from a woman. His curiosity got the best of him, so he opened it.

As soon as he read it, he realized what a big fucking mistake he'd made. It wasn't a letter, it was a goddamned landmine.

He closed his eyes and leaned his head against the back wall, trying to partway block out the noise around him. Right now there were enough seats to go around, but he wanted to make sure if that changed and there weren't enough for the women and children, he would know to get up and offer his place.

Children.

His mind wandered back to the conversation that he'd had with Gideon three days ago.

"I appreciate you seeing me off-hours," Nolan said for the third or fourth time.

"You know, you're really getting on my nerves, thanking me for something that you should expect from someone who is your teammate, let alone your friend."

Nolan raked his fingers through his dark hair as he considered Gideon's words.

"You're right."

"Fuck yeah, I'm right. Now, let's get down to it. What have you got for me?"

"An obituary and a letter."

"What do you want to start with?" Gideon asked. They were sitting in Gideon's tricked-out office in his bitching home there in Virginia Beach. Gideon probably had more computer hardware than NASA.

"The obituary. I don't have a print copy, but I found it online. It was in The Mountain Press Newspaper, the local one for the county where I grew up."

Gideon had it pulled up before Nolan finished speaking. "Is this the newspaper? Hold on, I found

O'Rourke. Ah, jeeze, she was young, Nolan. I'm really sorry for your loss."

Nolan's mouth twisted. "Yeah, well. Ginger wasn't much of a mom."

"Still..." Gideon's voice faded away as he gave Nolan a piercing look. When Nolan didn't say anything, Gideon turned back to a different keyboard. After two minutes of quiet, only broken by the sound of the keyboard clicking, Nolan spoke up.

"What are you doing?" Nolan asked.

"You said all you had was an obituary and a letter, right?"

Nolan nodded.

"I thought I would get more information on your mother, some background. I'm assuming it's been a while since you've been back home, right?"

Nolan felt his entire body tighten. Having Gideon probe was the last thing he wanted.

He rested his elbows on his knees, clasping his hands together.

"Nolan?" Gideon asked. "What is it? Do you want me to back off? I will if you want me to," Gideon said quietly.

"No, that's not it. I need you to do exactly that. It's just..." Nolan sat up straight and took a deep breath. "Ginger doesn't have the best track record. What you're going to find isn't going to be pretty."

"Like I said, man, I don't have to look."

"Yeah, you do. You *do* have to look. I haven't seen or talked to her since I left Jasper Creek when I turned eighteen. I never even looked her up online or anything. In the last few years, she started writing letters to me, and I've sent them all back, Return to Sender."

Gideon nodded like he understood.

Who knows, maybe he does.

"Nolan," Gideon asked almost gently. "Can I ask why you're opening this can of worms now?"

Nolan gritted his teeth. Again, his shoulders dropped and his elbows hit his knees. He stared at the floor for a moment, trying to get his shit tight. When he could finally look up, he could breathe. "I got a letter. Not from Ginger, from someone else."

Nolan reached into his back pocket and pulled out the worn envelope. Even though he'd only had it in his possession for a day and a half, he must have read it twenty times, and it was getting tattered.

"Here," he said as he handed Gideon the letter. "Read for yourself."

Gideon carefully accepted the envelope from Nolan's hand, then took the letter out of the envelope after looking at the front and the back. Nolan could see that he'd stopped for a moment on the butterfly sticker.

"Interesting."

He put the envelope on his desk after pulling out the letter. Nolan watched Gideon for any expression as he read the one sheet of lavender paper, but Gideon was stone-faced. When he finally looked up at Nolan he asked just one question.

"Do you believe what this Mary Smith is telling you?"

Nolan sifted his hand through his hair, pulling at it. "I haven't the foggiest idea. I looked it up. Mom, I mean Ginger, could have given birth, even at her age. She had me when she was fifteen. I just turned twenty-eight. That puts her at forty-three. They say it's rare, like a three percent chance, but with her shitty luck, it's definitely a possibility," Nolan said bitterly.

"Nolan, why are you so mad?"

"Because she's the last woman on earth who should ever be trusted with a kid." Nolan shot up out of his chair. "How could she have let this happen? And how in the hell did she bamboozle this Mary woman? How anyone would want to be friends with Ginger is beyond me."

"Calm down for a sec," Gideon said soothingly. "You said you left when you were eighteen. I get that it must have been a real bad situation, and you don't have to tell me anything. But that was ten years ago. Isn't it possible that your mother could have changed?"

"Gideon, that's the thing. She said she changed at least five times that I remember, and each time I had to go back to her, and I swear to God, she was eventually worse than she had been before I was pulled out." Nolan gripped the back of the chair where he'd been sitting. "So, no. There is no way she could have changed." He paused as he gave Gideon a considering look. "But maybe she had changed just long enough to fool this Mary woman. That's what she'd do with the social workers, that's why they'd send me back to her each time. Maybe that's what happened."

Gideon nodded. "Maybe it was."

Nolan stared off into space for a long time, reliving all those times when he was ripped away from a good family, a good situation, to be reunited with his mother. Those times were hell. Running away only made it worse.

He turned back to look at Gideon. "Go ahead and dig as deep as you need to. Not just on Ginger, but also on this Mary Smith woman." Nolan grinned for the first time since he arrived. "Who knows, Chief Petty Officer Gideon Smith? We might find out that Mary Smith is one of your long-lost cousins."

Gideon snorted. "I don't know. The way she said she has to leave and says her name is Mary Smith? She might as well call herself Jane Doe. I'm betting there isn't going to be any history for this woman."

"Yeah, that's my take too," Nolan sighed.

"Well, let's dig in."

―――――――

Nolan opened his eyes just a little as he heard the distinct sound of an older couple walking toward him.

"Honey, let's try to find you a seat over in one of the other agency areas. I'll come get you when they call our name," Nolan heard the old man say to his wife.

"Nonsense, I want to stay with you," she objected in a firm voice.

"Paula," he started.

Nolan stood up. "This seat is available," he told them. "I've been on planes too long today, I need to stretch my legs for a while."

"I can't take your seat, young man," Paula said.

Nolan frowned for a moment, then he smiled. "I'll tell you what, ma'am, you could do me a favor. Could you save my seat, so if I feel like sitting down again, it would be available to me?"

Her eyes lit up. "Well of course."

The old man, who was a foot taller than his wife, looked over her head and winked at Nolan. Nolan managed to keep a straight face and just gave him a chin lift in return, watching as he helped settle his wife into the chair.

CHAPTER TWO

She sat down at the library computer, positive that she'd timed it right. Iris had just been fed, so she would be out for at least two hours. This would give her time to check her e-mail while still checking in with her brother at their agreed-upon time.

It was a secure e-mail that Brian had set up for her. He said that nobody could access it and nobody knew about it. She'd only told four people about it, so she always liked checking it to see what they might have to say.

"Oops, outta time," she grinned. She was eager to chat with Brian. She'd check the e-mail after her chat with Brian was finished.

She logged into her WeChat account and was positive that Brian would be available because this was within their agreed-upon time to talk. Every other Tuesday between noon and three o'clock Pacific Standard Time.

She saw his message waiting out there.

Brian: *Maggie, talk to me.*

Maggie smiled. It was so good to be called by her real name. In the last two-and-a-half years she'd been known as Mia, Maya, Mila, and now Mary. She always used something close to Maggie so it was easy to respond to and there was less of a chance for her to screw up. As for her last name, she used something innocuous so the people she dealt with on the more disreputable websites would know she didn't want to be questioned. So far she'd been Jones, Johnson, Miller, and now Smith.

Maggie: *I'm here.* She added a happy face emoji and a heart emoji. *Everything is good so far. Nolan O'Rourke still hasn't contacted me.* She ended the sentence with a sad face emoji.

    Brian: *Damn, you've got to get out of there. You've stayed there too long, you know that, don't you?*

    Maggie: *I didn't think you were talking to anyone from Elk Bay. How do you know? What have you heard?*

    Brian didn't answer for a long time and Maggie had a bad feeling. A really bad feeling.

    Brian: *This time it wasn't Kyle who visited our*

father, it was Kyle's father. Said this was a stain on both our family and the VanWyck family. Said the marriage had to go through.

Maggie felt sick. She was getting colder and pulled her sweater tight around herself.

Brian: *Maggie, are you there?*

Maggie: *I'm here, do you know what our father said?*

Brian: *He agreed with Old Man VanWyck. He said it was time to bring you to heel.*

Maggie shuddered. How often had she heard that phrase before feeling the rod as a child? Not just her, but all of the Rutherford girls and her mother. In Elk Bay, Minnesota the man's word was law.

Maggie: *And our older brothers?*

Brian: *Paul was definitely in agreement, Peter didn't say much, just nodded. Paul said you were bringing shame to his family and to his in-laws.*

Maggie wanted to cry. She knew that one day her older brothers would turn on her, that they would become like her father, but she never thought they would take Kyle's side. They'd seen what he'd done to her.

Maggie: *What about Matthew?*

Brian: *He's staying out of it. I think his wife is having a positive influence on him.*

Maggie: *Are you getting this information from Laurel? It's not safe for her to be talking to you. If it's* *found out, they'll force her into marriage. Brian, you've got to stop it.*

Brian: *Don't worry big sister, we have a plan. And anyway, they're forcing her into marriage anyway, at Christmas. I'm getting her out of there right before Thanksgiving.*

Maggie: *Do you need help? Money?*

Brian: *Don't lie to me, you don't have money to give. But Maggie, this is serious. It's not just Kyle who's going to be coming for you now. Now it's going to be his father and his brothers. You're going to have to run again. You've stayed in Tennessee too long as it is.*

There was no way she could run. Not now, not without taking Iris with her, and she would never take Iris on the run with her. She looked down in the stroller and took solace in looking at the beautiful sleeping baby. She was so peaceful. The little girl didn't realize there was a storm brewing all around her.

Brian: *Talk to me, Maggie.*

Maggie: *I can't run. I can't leave Iris.*

Brian: *Kyle is nuts. He's been nuts since he was killing cats when we were kids. You don't want him around that baby. You need to get out of there.*

Nobody knew better than her what a psychopath Kyle VanWyck was. If it came down to it, she'd find a way to make sure that Iris was safe from him.

Brian: *Maggie, I'm serious. Remember what he did to Carla. He's home now. He thinks he has a lead. He said something about Branson, Missouri, said you were* *in some kind of Southern music town. What a dumbass. Pretty soon he's going to think of Nashville and set his sights on Tennessee.*

Maggie pulled her sweater even tighter.

Maggie: *I just can't bring myself to put her in foster care. What happens if she ends up in a family like ours?*

Her eyes began to sting. She had to hold herself together; she couldn't fall apart in the middle of the Jasper Creek library.

Brian: *I gave you O'Rourke's number, as well as his address. Haven't you called him?*

Maggie: *It goes to his voicemail and his voicemail is full. I wrote him a letter, but he hasn't answered back. I guess I'll have to talk to Trenda Avery and have her talk to her brother. Since they're both in the Navy he can talk to him, don't they all know one another?*

Brian: *No, Big Sister, they don't all know one another, but maybe he could track him down, it wouldn't hurt to try. Please, please, please think about leaving. Find someone there in Jasper Creek who'll take her. Do something. But you have to leave.*

Maggie had thought about asking Trenda to take Iris, but she couldn't. She knew the woman was still struggling to make ends meet just for her and her daughter Bella.

Brian: *I know we've talked about foster care before, and it scares you, but they do a really good job of* *screening people. What's more, she's young enough that somebody is sure to want to adopt her.*

Maggie's heart clenched. She looked down into the stroller. The idea of this little girl who had stolen her heart being raised by strangers killed her.

Brian: *I'm going to mail you some cash.*

Brian had left home before she did. Maggie knew he was working to get his social security card and driver's license. Everything was tough without a birth certificate. He was basically in the same shape she was. She refused to take any money from him. That wasn't what big sisters did. But he would send money if she didn't make him believe she was okay. So she was going to have to lie. Yep, she would have gotten the rod for sure three years ago if she'd lied.

Maggie: *I picked up some work here in town. It's honest work. I'm cleaning five different houses twice a month. The good thing is, they're paying me in cash and they let me bring Iris.*

Brian: *That's great.*

If they had been talking, Maggie knew she would've heard the relief in her brother's voice.

Maggie: *Do you think you'll have an update sooner than two weeks from now?*

Brian: *Yeah. Let's talk in a week, instead of two weeks. So next Monday, you good with that?*

Maggie: *I am. Thank you. I love you, little brother.*

Brian: *I love you, big sister. Stay safe.*

Maggie: *Always.*

Maggie leaned back in the unforgiving wooden library chair and tried like hell not to tear up. This was her life, it had been her life since Kyle VanWyck had decided he wanted to own her, and nothing was going to stop him. Running away before she married him was the smartest thing she'd ever done, no matter how furious her father might be. It was a matter of her survival.

Thank God for her baby brother, and thank God for him introducing her to the complexities of technology. She'd be lost without him.

She squeezed her eyes shut and willed herself not to cry, but it wasn't working. She looked down in the stroller and saw what *would* help. She touched Iris's soft cheek and put two fingers in front of her rosebud mouth so she could feel her breathing. That was better. Knowing the precious little girl was okay, made it all better.

Iris opened her electric blue eyes and stared at her.

"It's going to be all right, isn't it?"

Iris blew a bubble.

"I'll take that as a yes."

Mary turned back to her computer and went to check the e-mail account that Brian had set up for her. Soon her blood was running cold, and she was praying for a miracle.

It had taken four times longer to get his rental than it had to fly between Atlanta and Knoxville, but Nolan was doing his best to be Zen about the whole deal. He'd gotten the truck that he'd wanted, and he was on the road before nightfall.

It was growing chilly and the humidity just made it feel colder. If he were a reasonable man, he'd just stick to the heater in the rented truck. But he was back in Tennessee, where he'd grown up and first learned to drive. So, dammit, he wanted to have the window rolled down and his elbow on the ledge, especially when he was driving at dusk, so that's what he did.

Finally, he spotted the sign for Highway 321 and hit his blinker, then eased onto the familiar highway. His mind wandered as he drove past Pigeon Forge. That was where he'd first met Mrs. Sherman. He'd been able to stay with her, Mr. Sherman, and Michael for almost a year, before he'd been sent back to Ginger. They'd been nice. Too bad it hadn't lasted.

Whenever he saw either Formula One or a NASCAR race on TV, he always thought of the blanket that Mrs. Sherman had given to him and smiled. For just a second he was tempted to pull off the Highway and drive through town, maybe even drive past their old house, but he couldn't. He had a mystery to solve.

Next, he drove past Gatlinburg. Nothing to smile about there, so he sped up and carried on. Nolan took a deep breath and memories came rushing back. He was getting damn close to Jasper Creek—there was no sign

for it on the highway, but there was one for the
Cherokee National Forest and that's how he knew he
was close. He took that exit and one of the first things
he spotted was the sign for Polly's Restaurant. He
smiled, thinking about that piece of apple pie he'd had
when he'd first gone there.

Nolan kept going until he could no longer see
Polly's Restaurant in his rearview mirror, then forced
himself to keep on going until he hit the main drag of
Jasper Creek. Of course, it was named Chestnut Street,
since all streets were either a number or the name of a
tree. Mary said she lived in the same trailer park that
he'd spent a lot of his life trying to escape. Blue Ash
Village was four miles south of town and known by all
the local bullies as Blue Ass Village, and if you were
lucky enough to live there, you were often referred to as
one of the Blue Ass Village Idiots.

The closer and closer Nolan got to the mobile
home park, the more anxious he became, which was
preposterous. He was a grown man, and he'd been gone
for ten years. Why this should bother him so much, he
didn't have a clue. Maybe he should have checked into
the Whispering Pines hotel before coming here and
given himself a little more time to brace. But he knew
that would have been the coward's way out. And he
wasn't a coward, at least not anymore.

As soon as he pulled onto Ash Street, he could feel
the gravitational pull of the past tugging him forward.
Each numbered street he passed went higher and
higher until he was passing homes that should have

been condemned. But he knew they weren't because he could see clothes swaying on the laundry lines, and bikes and tricycles upended in the yards. When he saw the blue sign swinging in the distance, Nolan was amazed it was still hanging between the metal poles, but there it was.

Welcome To Blue Ash Village.

Nolan tried to tamp down all emotion. He wasn't able to stop the goosebumps that formed on his arms, but by God, he was able to take deep even breaths, so that was a win. The first little bit into the trailer park there were some decent doublewides, therefore management had bothered to pave the road just that little bit. But as soon as the nicer mobile homes stopped, so did the asphalt. Nolan started down the gravel road by rote. It took three turns, and there he was, in front of a white and light-blue trailer that looked tiny compared to his memories.

He shoved open the car door and got out.

Standing in front of his nightmare, overpowered by the smell of gin and cigarette smoke, Nolan started coughing. He covered his mouth with the crook of his elbow while his eyes watered. He turned and leaned his hands against the bed of the truck. After a couple of deep breaths, the smell dissipated. He turned around.

"Jesus," he sighed.

It had been a flashback. All he could smell now was the scent of pine trees.

Shit, Ginger, you're even haunting my sense of smell.

Nolan pressed his fingers against the bridge of his nose, trying his best to get his shit together. He kept his eyes closed for another few seconds, then opened them. He was intent on looking at his old home from the eyes of a trained operator who had been all over the world and survived. A man who had helped and saved numerous people and was no longer a victim.

Nolan let out an easy breath, then a second one, and opened his eyes. He looked at the plastic lattice fencing that surrounded the perimeter of the trailer. It was new. He didn't know why anybody bothered since it just surrounded a plot of dirt and clumps of dried dead weeds, and a crooked for rent sign stuck in the middle. He moved closer. The stairs had been repaired and they looked sturdy. There was even a handrail now.

He imagined a much older version of Ginger, pregnant, trying to get up the stairs into that tiny tin box of a house, especially during a hot, humid, Tennessee summer. He took in the front of the trailer and saw no sign of an air conditioner in any of the windows. Maybe there was one in back. Before he even knew he was going to look, he found himself circling the trailer. The only thing of note that he found were pink curtains with butterflies covering the window of the room that used to be his. Had Ginger started decorating a nursery for her daughter?

Nolan couldn't wrap his head around that. The woman he knew would never do something like that. His hand went to the back pocket of his jeans and pulled out the letter postmarked almost a month ago. He turned it over. Ginger might not do the decorating, but Mary Smith liked butterflies...

Seeing the curtains helped. It gave him distance between then and now, when there had just been a soiled pale green sheet covering the window. But that had been when he was eight. When he'd been reunited at different times, he'd changed things. He put up a dark blanket in winter and a clean white sheet in summer, purchases he'd made when he'd worked for Floyd at his gas station.

Enough stalling.

He looked down at the envelope one last time.

"Number Twenty-Eight, easy enough."

He stomped back to the truck, got in and took a right, and came to a trailer next to the lady who'd bought him pie. It almost seemed like an omen. *If you believed in that sort of thing.* Nolan shook his head.

He didn't pull up in front of the white mobile home, he drove by it and parked around the corner. Nolan wanted to take some time to surveil the place.

Shit, this trailer's even smaller than Ginger's.

He got out of the truck and walked down the back gravel alley where the bedrooms were usually tucked. But as he rounded the trailer he realized that the thing was just too thin, the bedrooms would be on either end. But maybe not even that. Maybe there was only one bedroom. He was tall enough to be able to peer inside, but he didn't want to be too obvious. The cheap metal blinds weren't for shit. Every third slat was either broken or missing, so if he peered inside and Mary was there, she'd be sure to spot him. He continued to round the trailer when he noticed the window at the end had the exact same butterfly curtains as Ginger's trailer.

Yep, it was definitely Mary Smith's trailer, and she definitely had Ginger's baby inside. What's more, based on everything Gideon had ferreted out, the baby belonged to Ginger Rose Hannity O'Rourke, which meant Iris Rose Hannity was his baby sister.

God help us both.

CHAPTER THREE

Nolan walked a little farther around the trailer and saw a piece-of-shit car underneath the dilapidated carport that looked like it was hanging off the side of the trailer using duct tape. He ducked underneath and got close to the dog-shit brown car. He found the name of the car since he didn't recognize the model. A Chevy Nova? Didn't they only come in cool-looking body styles, like old Mustangs? This must have been made in the mid-eighties. God, it was ugly. It probably didn't drive worth a damn either. He crouched down and peered underneath. Yep, there was a wet oil stain underneath it. Damn thing was on its last legs. When he stood up he peeked inside and saw a brand-new baby seat in the back. Well, Mary definitely had her priorities.

He heard the grate of the screen door opening.

"I've got a gun in one hand and my phone in the other. I just have to press one more digit, and the cops will be on the way. You better stop creeping around and tell me who the hell you are."

Nolan stood still. There was no fear in the voice, just calm determination. He didn't doubt the part about the gun, but he wondered if a woman living off the grid would really call the cops.

"I'm Chief Petty Officer Nolan O'Rourke."

"Since you've already been peeking into my windows, you know your way around. So, go ahead and put your ID up against the kitchen window, but don't make any sudden moves."

He heard the screen door shut, as well as the interior door.

Interesting. This didn't seem like the woman who had sent him the letter. She'd seemed open and welcoming. *What had happened?* He looked around and realized that it was now dark, and there weren't any lights in the park. The only light was her front porch light, which wasn't putting out a lot of lumens.

"What's taking you so long?" she shouted.

Nolan pulled his wallet out of his back pocket and pulled out his driver's license and his military ID card, then stuffed his wallet back into his jeans pocket. As he turned the corner to the front of the trailer he heard a baby start to cry.

He heard movement in the trailer, then a soothing voice that sounded nothing like the surly woman who'd been threatening him with a gun. Nolan went to the front of the trailer and pressed his ID against the window with one hand, keeping the rest of his body well away from the window. He really didn't want to be shot by mistake.

Nolan winced as the baby's cries turned to out-and-out screams.

What's wrong with her?

Then the screaming stopped as suddenly as it had started. He heard the door unlock and open. A petite, red-headed woman appeared, holding a baby.

"I was afraid you weren't going to come." She tilted her head to indicate Nolan should come inside, then she turned around and headed to the kitchen. "Take a seat, anywhere."

Nolan didn't know what he was expecting, but the ratty furniture didn't come as any kind of a shocker. The smell of vanilla and talcum powder was an unexpected surprise though. A welcome surprise.

Nolan looked over his seating choices. There wasn't much room in the tiny trailer, but what room there was, she'd made use of. She had put colorful blankets over a worn couch that was probably second- or third-hand. He could see where the stuffing was coming out on the arms. Then there were the two chairs that were even worse. Not only did they have stuffing coming out of the arms and doilies decorating their backs, but towels were also tucked over the seat cushions.

Just how bad are those cushions underneath the towels?

He chose to sit on one of the two rickety barstools

against the kitchen counter so he could watch what she was doing.

Relieved didn't even begin to cover how Mary felt. It was like a two-ton weight had been lifted off her shoulders now that Ginger's son had arrived. Iris would have a place to stay, because after that e-mail, she needed to get out of town, like yesterday.

"Now that you're down to a medium roar, I can get your dinner handled. How does that sound, Sweet Pea?"

Out of the corner of her eye, she saw Nolan staring at Iris, but she wasn't going to make a big deal of it.

"What do you think? Do you want formula out of the bottle with the kitties on it this afternoon, or can I interest you in some formula out of the bunny bottle?"

Iris's little legs pumped when she'd said kitty. "Okay, so kitty it is."

Mary couldn't help herself. She cuddled Iris closer, pressed a kiss into her fat little neck rolls, and Iris gave a happy little gurgle. "Aren't you a love?"

Mary plucked the kitty bottle out of the cupboard, then the can of formula. She measured out the amount of formula she needed into the bottle, then plucked an unopened bottle of water off the counter and gave it a woeful stare. Normally she would have brought Iris's infant seat with her and placed it on the counter so she could watch and entertain her while she got her meal ready. Doing it one-handed was tough, because she sure couldn't open the bottle of water. Maggie sighed.

"Do you need help?" Nolan asked in that rumbly Southern-accented voice of his.

"Yeah, I do." Mary walked around the counter with the bottle of water. Nolan reached out and Mary slid Iris into the crook of his arm.

"Be careful to support her head."

"Wait a minute, I meant—"

Mary gave a half chuckle. "I know what you meant, but you're on baby duty. It'll be faster if you hold her for me while I fix her lunch. You don't mind, do you?" She knew he did, but she highly doubted that the big bad Navy man would admit to it.

"No. No, I don't mind." Nolan looked down at Iris like she was a bomb waiting to go off. His arm was so stiff that Iris started to fuss again.

"You need to relax, Nolan." She put down the bottle of water, then gripped his upper arm and elbow. "Like this." Mary bent his arm a little more so that it was curved, and then pressed his forearm closer to Iris so that she was tucked in closer to his chest.

Then she saw it happen. Iris stopped fussing. Instead, she started staring up into the eyes of the new human. She was entranced, and so was Nolan.

He stared down at his little sister like he'd never seen a pair of eyes before. Maybe he hadn't. Not ones that looked identical to his own. Mary was surprised that sparks of lightning didn't pass between them since they both had such electric blue eyes. She'd spent hours studying Iris's blue eyes as they'd turned from the original darker baby blue into a lighter shade with a hint of yellow around the pupils that made them look like the sun was shining behind them. And now Nolan was doing the same thing.

She picked up the bottle of water and quietly went back to her task of mixing the formula then heating the bottle up by running it under warm tap water, careful not to get the sterilized nipple wet. When she looked up from what she was doing, she found that both Iris and Nolan were staring at her.

"She likes you," he said. "I mean she likes watching you. Of course, she loves you. You're her mom." He stopped. "I didn't mean that. Not really. But you're the only mom she's known."

Mary felt herself flush.

"I call myself Aunt Mary." But when it was just the two of them she called herself Auntie Maggie. Uncomfortable, she looked down at the bottle in her hand. "Do you want to feed her?" she asked.

"I'm not sure," Nolan said tentatively.

Mary looked up and smiled. "Come on, Navy Man, it's easy. Trust me, she'll show you what she wants. Come sit down in the chair. I'll get you a pillow to rest your arm so you won't get tired."

Nolan lifted an eyebrow and she frowned.

"What?"

"Honey, I think my arm will be able to handle holding this little bundle without needing to rest it on a pillow."

"Oh." It was all she could think to say. "I kind of didn't think that through, did I?"

"I'm thinking you're not used to men, is all."

The flash of a fist connecting with her jaw came out of nowhere.

Mary jerked backward, trying to avoid the inevitable next punch. Her ponytail swung and hit her in the face, and she cried out at the sting. She heard a thump and she jumped again, this time hitting the side of her knee against the coffee table. She hissed in pain.

She was met with dead silence, then a whimper from Iris.

"Easy, girl," a soothing Southern voice said. Mary didn't know if it was directed at Iris or her.

She shook her head and touched her jaw. It stung, but didn't hurt, not as if she'd taken a punch—she *knew* what that felt like. She was still having trouble focusing. Processing.

"Are you with me now?" Again, that distinct Southern accent. So different from what she was used to. She nodded and touched her cheek again and realized that the sting had come from her own hair.

"Mary, will you say something?"

She looked up and saw Iris's blue eyes staring at her from a man's face.

Nolan. Nolan O'Rourke.

Oh, God. A flashback. I'm an idiot.

"Mary, talk to me." He sounded freaked. Freaked but kind.

"I'm fine," she murmured. She dropped her gaze

and stared at the floor, not wanting to look up. Afraid his kindness might morph into confusion or disappointment. Then she saw it. She'd dropped Iris's bottle. A little bit of formula had dribbled out of the nipple. Her stomach clenched. The formula cost an arm and a leg, and she'd just wasted it on her foolishness. She bent down and picked up the bottle.

"Do you want to rinse that off and give it to me?" Nolan asked gently.

Mary took a deep breath and looked at the man's face. He didn't look upset, shocked—or even worse, all sympathetic and stuff—like she might have expected. It was as if his face was set in neutral, and she relaxed.

"Honey, Sweet Pea is getting restless, I think she wants her bottle," Nolan said again. Still, he was talking to her in a calm voice. It reminded her of a still lake she'd seen when she'd been in Idaho at Carla's. So still, it had been a sanctuary for a little while.

"Mary?" he prompted again.

"I have to make up a new bottle. This one isn't sterile anymore."

"What do you mean?" Nolan looked confused.

"The nipple has touched the linoleum. She can't have this. It's very important that babies this little only have sterile food, that's why I use bottled water to mix the formula."

"Why not just put on a new nipple?"

"Maybe some of the formula spilled out, but then leaked back into the bottle from the hole in the nipple. I can't risk it."

Nolan held out his free hand and Mary reluctantly handed him the bottle in question.

He examined the bottle and nipple. "Honey, this nipple is tight as a drum. The only reason any formula hit the floor is because it hit so hard. Trust me, no formula, and certainly nothing from the floor, got back into the bottle. You're good. Just put on another nipple and we're good to go."

"Are you sure?" Mary tugged at the end of her ponytail, weaving her fingers through the ends of her hair.

"Positive. I think you're doing a fantastic job with this little lady, but on this one, you might be going a tad bit overboard."

She saw the twinkle in his eye. And she blew out a breath. He was teasing her. It was going to be all right. "Only a tad bit?" she asked.

"Okay, you've high jumped past tad bit, and you've pole-vaulted into crazy paranoid. How's that?"

Mary stifled a giggle and couldn't believe it. Not after having a flashback like the one she'd just had. She went and put a different nipple on the baby bottle. By the time she got back, Nolan had taken off his leather jacket and she was met with him in a gray t-shirt that lovingly molded to his muscles. Thank God he was looking the other way, otherwise, he would see the way she was staring. His large, strong body was both a good thing and a bad thing. He turned to look at her.

"Is the bottle ready?"

Mary nodded and showed Nolan where to sit

down. She also gave him a burp towel. "Sometimes Iris will drink too much, and then erp it up."

"*Erp?*"

"I like that word better than vomit."

"Hate to tell you, but 'erp' isn't a word," Nolan said as he scootched down into the chair and cuddled Iris close. As soon as he pressed the nipple close to her mouth, she latched on like a bear to honey.

"Look at that," he said in awe. "She just goes for it."

"She's a strong eater. That's the reason she's grown so fast."

"What do you mean, grown so fast? She's a tiny little thing. Shouldn't she be bigger for three months?"

"No, actually she was above the norm for a baby her age when I took her in to the pediatrician last week."

Nolan lifted his gaze from Iris and stared up at Mary. "Why'd you have to take her to the doctor, was she ill?"

"Oh no, that was just her three-month check-up. It was normal. The doctor said she's thriving."

"Hmmm," he said as he turned his attention back down to the baby.

Mary would have given anything to know what that 'hmmm' meant, but then again maybe she didn't, so she didn't ask.

She watched as Iris did one of her favorite things. While she was drinking from her bottle, she grabbed at Nolan's hand and seized one of his fingers. Nolan was startled and his head shot up to look at her.

"She has a phenomenal grip. Is she supposed to be this strong?" Nolan asked.

Mary couldn't stop her giggle.

"Why are you laughing?" Nolan didn't understand.

"Have you been around babies much?"

"Yeah. I'm the team medic. I don't have pediatric training, but I've been to places in this world where I was the closest thing anyone had to a pediatrician. So, I've given inoculations, antibiotics, dealt with kids and babies who've had things as easy as an earache, to typhoid fever and malaria."

"Nolan, I had no idea you had a medical background, that's amazing. But maybe it's because you've been around mostly sick babies, that you don't realize that most healthy babies are this strong."

"My teammate, Sebastian Durand had a son last year, I was over at his home a while back, so I saw Neil."

"Did you hold him?"

"Yep. He had the croup, so I was over there assuring Sebastian and Gianna that Neil was going to be fine. I remember thinking that Neil looked tiny in his daddy's arms. But now that I'm holding Iris, Neil looked gigantic. So, you're sure the pediatrician said she's fine? She seems small for an American baby. I mean it's great she's so hungry. Nothing will break your heart more than when a baby is too weak from hunger to eat, but, see how she's sucking down this bottle? She's desperate for food. When I try to pull it out of her mouth just a little bit, she grabs at it. See?" He tried it again and turned down anxious eyes at the baby girl when her hands moved to touch the bottle.

"She knows what she wants," Mary smiled. "I swear to you, Nolan, she's meeting all the milestones just fine. As a matter of fact, when I took her to the pediatrician, she was a pound over the weight they expected." Mary reached over Nolan's shoulder and gently pulled at Iris's foot. "You're a little piglet, aren't you, Sweet Pea?"

The baby pulled her foot away from Mary and let go of the bottle, bunching her hands into little fists.

Nolan laughed. "I don't think she liked being called a piglet."

"That's her way of telling us she's getting full." Mary watched as Iris spit out the nipple and turned her head. Her fists unclenched and her eyes closed as she relaxed even more in Nolan's arms.

"She's beautiful."

"Yes, she is. I'm impressed that Iris was willing to let you hold her and showed no fear. She cries when she is scared and doesn't like somebody new."

"You've had her around new people? Who?"

"Her pediatrician. I know she didn't like Dr. Ryan. She had a fit when he tried to listen to her heart."

"Maybe it was the shots," Nolan suggested. "The kids never much liked me after I stuck them either."

Iris wrinkled her nose up at him. Mary could swear she was agreeing with him. "Yeah, you didn't like getting your shots, did you?"

"Nolan, she started crying long before she got her

shots," Iris laughed. "I'm serious, I just wanted you to get used to her, I wasn't expecting her to take to you so easily. You have the touch. Take the towel I gave you and put it over your shoulder."

"Like this?" he asked.

Mary nodded.

"Now carefully bring up Iris so she's resting on your shoulder. Then you're going to lightly tap and rub her back. That will help get her to relieve herself of any gas she might have built up during her feeding. We don't want her to get a tummy ache when we put her to bed."

Once again Mary watched as Nolan looked down at Iris, and she saw his face soften with a look of utter amazement. He stroked her forehead, and reverently touched her downy red hair. "What do you say, Sweet Pea, are you ready to vomit on me?"

Iris didn't open her eyes. Instead, she just rubbed her nose and rolled closer to her big brother's chest.

Nolan carefully moved Iris into the correct position so that she was resting on his shoulder. He started to gently pat the baby and once again the little girl snuggled closer to the man. She moved her head so that her lips were touching his neck.

"Nolan, you need to move the towel," Mary warned.

"What?"

It was too late. Iris let out a mighty belch for such a tiny human, and Mary's mouth opened in horror and laughter as she saw the milky puke running down the inside of Nolan's t-shirt.

"You know, Iris, many a SEAL has tried to out-belch another, but I think you might just win the contest," he said as he chuckled. He looked up at Mary. "Do I need to keep rubbing her back, or is she done now?"

"Oh, I think she's done. It's time for her nap. I'll just check her diaper and put her down. That can give you time to get cleaned up. The bathroom is right before the bedroom, on the left."

"Got it."

She saw him watch her squeeze around the sofa so she could get to the changing table. With Iris so sleepy, changing her diaper was a breeze. He continued to stare.

"Do you want to learn how to change her diaper?"

"No," he held up his hands. "Not ready for that yet. Just taking it all in." He turned and headed to the bathroom.

CHAPTER FOUR

Ever since living with the Shermans, Nolan knew how tiny trailer bathrooms were. But Mary's bathroom had to be the smallest on the market, smaller than the one in Ginger's trailer that was for sure. He had to scrunch his shoulders inward just to take off his tee.

There was a knock on the door.

"Nolan, there's a little bin on the other side of the toilet with some washcloths and towels. You can use those to clean up."

He looked down at the lavender washcloth and picked it off the top of the pile. He grinned when he saw the yellow butterfly embossed in the corner. It was a good thing she told him the linens were there, he would have missed them in this cramped space. He used the cloth to wipe up the formula residue that had dripped down his neck and chest. Then he rinsed the portion of his t-shirt that needed cleaning. He wrung it out and grabbed a hand towel, dried himself off, and got dressed.

Not bad, he thought as he looked in the mirror. He stopped for a moment and stared.

Shit, my eyes look like hers.

He leaned forward and widened his eyes so he could take a good look. He'd never really thought much about his eyes. Once or twice he'd hear people say he had his mother's baby blues, but that was it. Yeah, a few women in his life would comment on them, but it meant nothing. But now?

He knew his eyes were light blue, but he'd never really noticed that there were weird little yellow starbursts coming out from his pupil. It made them look lighter. Brighter. Iris had the same thing. It made her eyes seem almost electric.

Shit.

He stepped away from the mirror and hung the towel and washcloth over the shower door so they could dry, then stepped sideways to let himself out.

When he stepped back into the main living area he took a long look. This place was at least two or three hundred square feet smaller than Ginger's trailer. It was ridiculous.

"Why aren't you living in Ginger's trailer? It's bigger. With Iris, you could use the extra room, couldn't you?"

She was behind the couch again doing something at the changing table, probably cleaning. She kept her head down as she answered. "Your mom was really late with her rent. I mean *really* late. While she was in the hospital, the owner cleaned out the trailer and just threw everything she owned out into the yard then changed her locks." Nolan wasn't sure, but he thought he caught a glimmer of tears forming in her eyes.

He tried to remember who owned Ginger's trailer, but he came up blank.

"Who in the hell would do something that shitty?"

"This place is owned by a corporation. The couple that runs the place only comes around every week. None of us know where they live, they just show up." She didn't look him in the eye, instead, she focused on folding stuff on top of the changing table. "They're not very nice," she said in a quiet voice.

"Goddamn right, they're not very nice. What happened to mom's stuff?"

"Some of the neighbors grabbed it and saved it. I was so thankful when I came back here and found out. Especially all of the stuff that I'd bought for Iris."

"*You* bought?"

Again, she dipped her head so he couldn't see her expression. "I mean, *we* bought. Your mom and I went shopping together to get her things like her crib, changing table, car seat, infant seat, some onesies, diapers, and stuff. You know."

"Onesies? No, I don't know, explain it to me."

"It doesn't matter. Most of it's here."

"Tell me the names of the couple."

She looked up fast. "For what reason? It's done now."

Nolan felt a headache coming on. He rubbed the back of his neck.

"What about her car? Yours is a piece of shit. Couldn't you be driving Ginger's?"

"She sold hers to make rent when I ran out of savings."

"Jesus, Mary. Just how much did she take you for?"

"What are you talking about?" She glared at him, her voice indignant. "Your mother didn't take me for a dime. I willingly helped her. She was one of the nicest people I've ever met."

Nolan snorted. "Yeah, sure. Now tell me how much she was into you for."

"Nothing. I didn't loan her a dime."

"Yeah, like I don't know this game. Usually, she played it on men, though. So how much did you *give* her?" He raised his hands and used his fingers to make air quotes around the word 'give'.

"I told you, I didn't do anything I didn't want to. I'm a big girl. I am more than capable of making my own decisions. I really don't appreciate your tone."

Nolan put his fists on his hips and really looked around the room.

Every third slat on the window blinds was missing, and he'd already seen what was going on with the cupboards. He looked up, and just as he suspected, there were water stains on the ceiling, and he'd bet his bottom dollar that the roof leaked when it rained. The place was a hovel, and here she was saying she didn't mind giving money to Ginger?!

What the fuck!

"Mary, you do realize you didn't have to do a damn thing for her, right?"

Mary shoved her hands on her hips too and practically growled, "Nolan, you do realize that I can do whatever darn thing I want with my money, right?"

"And where has that left you?"

She flew around the couch like she'd grown wings. "Now listen here, you big ape," she hissed. "I don't want to wake Iris, otherwise I'd be screaming at the top of my lungs, so just assume I am, okay? You haven't been around for ten darn years. You don't know the story. I've read the letters you sent back to Ginger, that's how I knew to trace you, and yeah, I can see that Ginger was a royal jerkface to you. Royal. Like she could have worn a crown. But that's not the woman I knew. That's not the woman who nurtured Iris in her body and had big dreams for her. She was an entirely different woman, so don't you tell me what I should and shouldn't have done with my money. You got that?"

Nolan damn near laughed when she poked him in the chest with her tiny finger. Seriously, she was like a little pissed-off pixie. He took a deep breath. Then another, and saw that Mary was doing the exact same thing.

"I'm sorry," they said simultaneously.

"I was out of line," they both said at the same time again.

This time they laughed.

"Let me talk, Honey," Nolan said. "Yeah, I still

have mommy issues, I will admit that freely, at least to you since you've seen all the letters I've returned to her." He rubbed the back of his neck.

Fuck. Mommy issues. How fucking pathetic.

She stopped poking her finger into his chest and placed her hand over his heart instead, like she was trying to offer him comfort.

"Nolan, it's understandable, what with—"

"Mary, let's not get into that, okay? Let's focus on what you and Iris need. That's what's most important right now."

Her hand dropped and she took a step backward. "What Iris needs is a good home."

"Yeah, and this isn't it. I'm sorry, I'm not trying to be mean, but this isn't a good environment for you to be living in, let alone a baby. What's more, it's not safe. I know you feel that way, otherwise, you wouldn't have met me at the door with a gun."

"It's fine."

Nolan took another look around the trailer. "It's cold." Now that the sun was completely down and it was dark outside, he was noticing it. He looked at Mary and saw that she had put on another sweater on top of the sweater she was already wearing, the sleeves pulled down so that only her fingertips were showing.

"If you're this cold, how is Iris doing?"

"I have a space heater in my bedroom. That's where her crib is at."

"You should have one out here too."

"There's no need. When it's cold like this, I just go

to my room. No need to have two space heaters running at the same time." She smiled up at him.

Now came the touchy part. Nolan knew damn good and well how and when she came to be in this shitty trailer. She'd popped up at Blue Ash Village thirteen months ago and was subletting this tin can for double the amount that she should be. According to what Gideon had been able to rustle up, the people who owned the trailer lived in Texas and had been subletting it for years. They preferred cash and always advertised on one of the less reputable online classified ads search engines. It was a site where the cops were always trolling to find stolen property. She'd been doing okay while she worked under the table at Polly's Restaurant and Rowdy's Roadhouse on the outskirts of Gatlinburg. At least she had been, until a little over three months ago when she had to quit working days at Polly's and dropped to only two nights a week at Rowdy's.

"Were you going to say something?" Mary asked.

"Hell, I'm crap at subtlety. At least when something's important. And dammit, this is important. Mary, I know that you don't have any money. I have a friend who is great with computers and he found out how much you're paying for this dump, and the fact that you're no longer working at Polly's and only part-time at Rowdy's. I know you've got to be damn near down to your last dime."

The color drained out of her face.

"I know, I know, now you're upset. I knew you

would be. But the sooner we get down to the bottom of things, the easier it's going to be to fix them. You are doing an amazing job with that little girl in there," he said pointing down the hall. "You're her mother. A mother that she is lucky to have. But you're on the run, and you can't afford to take care of her when you're trying to live off the grid. That's why you reached out to me. I can help."

Instead of the smile he was hoping for, he watched aghast as tears dripped down her face.

"Mary. Don't you understand? This is a good thing."

"I prayed you'd come. I prayed so hard," she whispered as she swiped at her wet cheeks. Mary leaned back against the arm of one of the old, tattered chairs as if she had lost the power to stand.

That was good. She didn't sound mad, at least. "Honey, you're shivering. Either you need to get to bed, or you need to come with me."

He watched as she gave a reluctant nod without looking up. He couldn't stand it. What was she thinking, had he royally fucked it all up? He gently pressed his knuckles underneath her chin and lifted her face so that he could see her eyes.

"Wouldn't a night away from here be a good thing?"

She looked so lost. So young.

"Where would we go?"

Nolan pulled out his cell phone from his back pocket. He always plugged in hotels, rental agencies, restaurants, everything really, before he went anywhere. He never knew when he might need to get in touch with the facility.

He touched the side of his phone and said, "Whispering Pines Hotel," and was soon connected.

Mary wasn't crying anymore. Instead, she looked confused. A woman came onto the line and greeted him.

"Hello, my name is Nolan O'Rourke. I have a room reserved through Monday. I was wondering if I could bump that up to a suite if you have any available. Preferably something with two bedrooms."

He waited while the woman clicked away at her keyboard.

"Mr. O'Rourke, we do have a suite available. It's going to be two and a half times your current rate." He gave an internal wince, but then gave thanks to the fact that he was a saver and not a spender, so he had money to throw at this problem.

"That sounds good. I'll take it. Do you have any problem with us bringing our baby along?"

"Not at all, this is a family-friendly hotel. Do you need us to bring up a crib to your room?"

"That would be great." Nolan grinned. "We'll be there within the hour. Also, I know that you don't have room service, but could you recommend a restaurant that might deliver at this hour?"

"We have a local diner called Polly's. They don't deliver, but you could pick up a to-go order on your way to the hotel."

"Good idea," Nolan agreed. "Thanks for all the help."

He hung up and waited for Mary to say something. He didn't have to wait long.

"The Whispering Pines? A suite? I heard what she said. Are you rich or something? That's crazy, Nolan."

"It's not a problem. We need to get shit figured out, and this will give both of us some breathing space. How about you pack up what's needed for you and Iris til Monday. I'll grab the car seat out of your car, and we'll put it in my truck."

"That won't work. If you want me to stay there for more than a couple of days, I'm going to need my car. I have to drive into Gatlinburg for my job on Friday."

"Can't you call in sick?"

"I've already missed too much time as is. I'll be fired for sure if I miss more."

Nolan rubbed the back of his neck—the kinks were coming back in earnest. She didn't know it, but there wasn't a chance in hell she was driving her POS to Gatlinburg by herself whenever she had to go in. What's more, he wanted to make sure that everyone knew that she had a protector.

"Okay, we'll drive both cars."

"Does your truck have a backseat?" she asked.

"Yeah. Why?"

"I'd feel safer if Iris rode with you. Your rental is probably safer than my car. I'm not sure that the airbags even work in mine."

"Jesus, Mary," he growled.

She held out her hand, palm facing him. "I don't want to hear it. Everything has worked out so far, and if you had read any of your mom's letters, then you would have known what was going on," she growled back at him.

She was a feisty little pixie.

CHAPTER FIVE

Mary sank down lower in the bathtub. It was heaven. She'd never bathed in such a big tub, this was such a luxury. Even though she'd gotten to use a bath while she'd been on the run, she never took it for granted. When she lived at home a bath was a few-and-far-between perk, so this was heaven. Nolan had promised he'd handle Iris if she woke up, and Mary intended to take him at his word. It was a shame that she didn't have anything nicer to put on when she got out of the bath.

She thought back to how she'd grown up in Elk Bay, Minnesota. There'd only been one bathroom with a bathtub, and to save on heating bills, her father had been very strict about allowing anyone to have a bath. Not that her brothers cared, but her two older sisters were just as upset as she was, and Catherine was too vocal about it. Mary winced, thinking about the trouble her older sister would get into for backtalking.

I'm in Tennessee—concentrate on the present.

Mary picked up the shampoo that the hotel had provided. She'd never heard of the brand, but it smelled divine. She poured it into her hands and started to lather her hair, rejoicing in the soft feel and heady scent. Catherine and Ruth would love this, too bad she couldn't send them some. Of course, Ruth's husband would force her to throw it away. God, she missed her sisters. Before she started getting sad, she dunked her head under the faucet to rinse the shampoo out of her hair.

The bath had made her slippery since she'd used a mega amount of bath salts, so she was careful stepping out onto the pretty tile floor. She covered herself with a towel as fast as she could so she wouldn't have to see her ribcage in the mirror. Even after two and a half years, the scar was still raised, red, and puckered. *Ugly. So ugly.*

"Mary?"

Her towel slipped when she jumped.

"Is everything okay? What's wrong with Iris?" Mary clutched her towel even tighter.

"Nothing's wrong with her. She's just fine. Polly's is closing soon, and I wanted to know what you'd like me to order for you, and then I'll go pick it up."

Like Pavlov's dog, her stomach growled. She tried to think of the last time she ate something but came up blank. The idea of one of Polly's turkey sandwiches with cranberry sauce and extra mayo sounded wonderful!

"I'll be right there."

"Take your time. Don't slip. If your bathroom is anything like mine, those tiles look slippery as hell."

"I won't."

She listened and breathed a sigh of relief when she heard her bedroom door shut. Still, that didn't mean anything, he could still be in her bedroom, and he could have just shut the door to fake her out.

Stop it! Stop measuring every man by the Kyle yardstick.

She grabbed the sleeping jammies she'd brought in. They were warm, dull, and thick. No man could find her attractive in these.

Not that I want Nolan to find me attractive!

She felt herself start to blush.

Once her clothes were on, she went back to the bathroom. It was safe to look in the mirror. Her hair was going to be a tangled mess if she slept with it wet, but she didn't have time to blow dry it. Even though she hated them because they reminded her of home, she quickly put her hair into one long braid. That would take care of her problem for the night. She went out into the suite's common area.

Before she could even say anything, Nolan was handing her his phone.

"I've called up the menu. Tell me what you want, and I can call in the order. Polly hasn't joined the twenty-first century, so no ordering online. So I guess we're lucky that somebody made a picture of the menu and put it up on Polly's Google page."

"I did that. It's as far as Polly would let me go," Mary said with a shrug. "However, it did increase the number of pick-up orders she started to receive. It even got to the point that she was willing to take some phone orders herself without hanging up on people."

Nolan laughed. "I could see her doing that. She never suffered fools easily."

"No, sir. It was touch and go in the beginning, whether I would last. She said I was too timid, but working nights at Rowdy's took the timid right on out of me."

Nolan frowned. "You're really a tiny little thing."

"I'm not a thing," Mary protested immediately. She'd been treated like property in the past and she was never letting that happen again.

"I'm sorry. Come to think about it, that is a bad phrase, but I didn't mean it that way, I promise. You're just pint-sized, but you're a firecracker."

Mary sighed. "Can't I just be a woman?"

She watched as he rubbed the back of his neck and decided to let him off the hook. "Let me call in the order. I know what I want. What do you want?"

"I can't decide between the country-fried pork chops or the catfish," Nolan admitted.

Mary nodded. "I've got this."

She dialed a number into his phone, smiling when it was Kathy who answered. "Hey, Kath, it's Mary. Yeah, I'm looking to order two dinners, but I need to know if Slim's cooking tonight."

"Yes he is, and he's screwing up everybody's fish

orders. He can't cook a fillet to save his life," Kathy answered.

Mary laughed. "Ain't that the truth? Okay, here's the order, you ready?"

"Girl, I was born ready."

"I need the chops." She looked up at Nolan. "What sides you want?"

"The cheesy grits and the mash potatoes," he answered.

"I need grits and mash on the side, don't skimp on the gravy, he's a big boy."

"He is, is he? You have something to tell Auntie Kathy? You been holding out?"

"You get this order right, I might be willing to share," Mary tossed back.

"Okay, sweetie, and can I guess what you want?"

"Go for it," Mary dared her friend.

"You want the turkey sandwich on the potato roll, with extra turkey, mayo, and cranberry. Then you want a side of broccoli and a side of mac. How'd I do?"

"You didn't get my drink or my dessert."

"Sweet tea, and a slice of chocolate cake."

"You nailed it, Kathy. Hold on and I'll find out what Nolan wants."

She looked over at Nolan, expecting him to be ready to name his drink and dessert, but realized he hadn't heard Kathy's side of the conversation.

"Nolan, what would you like to drink? I'm getting sweet tea; if you want that, we can just ask for a jug. Then I need to know what you want for dessert."

He shook his head. "You really have this down, don't you?"

"You can't work as a waitress for ten months without doing things fast. So what'll it be?"

"Sweet tea, jug," he answered. "I would say warm apple pie and vanilla ice cream, but it would be a melted mess by the time I brought it back to the hotel."

"Nah," she waved a hand at him. "Kathy can set you up."

"Kath, make that a jug of sweet tea, plenty of lemons, sugar, and none of that fake stuff. He wants apple pie and vanilla ice cream, but do it up right."

"Will do. I'll put this in right now. It'll be ready by the time he gets here from your trailer."

"He's coming from Whispering Pines, so see if you can make it faster."

"Fancy, fancy. Yep, Auntie Kathy wants to know alllll about this."

Mary laughed for the first time that day. *God Bless Kathy Ayers.*

Luckily business had been real busy at Polly's when Nolan had got there. Apparently, people had just left the movies in Gatlinburg and had decided to come to Polly's for a late dinner or dessert. He was still raw from memories as it stood—he didn't need to see Polly or anyone else from his past just yet.

"You Nolan?" A middle-aged woman with steel

gray hair asked him. She had a piercing gaze that she trained on him. He could tell that she was someone who had Mary's back, and he was glad to see it.

"I am," he answered.

"We got slammed at the last minute. Your order is going to take another five to ten, you okay with that?"

Nolan nodded.

"Go to one of the barstools and Polly or Jeff will set you up with a tea or a soda while you wait."

Fuck.

He walked past the red hostess stand and across the black and white checked floor to the stainless steel and white counter. The barstools were still the cheap red Naugahyde that he remembered. He saw Polly chatting with someone on the right end of the bar, so he chose the left end. It was then he realized he was almost on top of the booth where he'd had his first piece of apple pie a la mode.

He thought back to that day as he seated himself up on the barstool. It had been one of the hottest days of summer, and he didn't have anything to do or any friends to do nothing with, so he was sitting up in his favorite climbing tree. An old lady who lived in the same trailer park where he grew up had called him out of the old maple. He was sure he was going to get yelled at, but instead, she said she'd take him to Polly's Diner.

He'd been confused, but she was a grown-up and since she hadn't yelled at him, and she'd always been nice to her cat, he decided to go with her. She made him put on a seatbelt, and her car smelled good, and when he told her that, she explained it was because of the little tree that hung from the mirror.

She took him to Polly's and introduced him to a woman named Polly. Somehow, the lady knew his name was Nolan O'Rourke, and even said he was Ginger Hannity's boy. Polly said that in that case, he deserved two scoops of ice cream on his pie. He'd never had pie before. When Polly brought out the two plates, he'd been disappointed because his ice cream was already melting, but the lady somehow knew he was kind of mad about it, and told him to take a bite anyhow. That's when he found out how good hot apple pie with cold vanilla ice cream was. It was the best thing in the whole world.

The lady took him home and told him that he was strong, and that was good. The next day Nolan watched as some man who kind of looked like her came with a big orange truck and took all of her stuff out of her house and packed it away. He continued watching as she carried her cat in a little box with a handle. He waved goodbye to her and she smiled back. He never found out her name.

"Were you thinking you could sneak on in here and not say 'hey' to me?" Polly demanded to know.

Nolan gave her a slow smile, at the same time berating himself for not noticing her coming up on him. God, this whole trip had him off-kilter.

"It was a shame about your mama passing the way she did. She was expecting it, but all of us were hoping she could beat the odds."

He frowned as he looked at a woman who had always been larger than life. The entire time he'd known Polly Watson she'd never had anything good to say about Ginger O'Rourke.

Polly slapped her hand down on the counter.

"You don't know, do you?"

"Know what?"

"How your mother was one of the rare few who turned their life around. God knows how she managed to do it in this small town, especially when you consider her parents did their level best to grind her into the dirt for so many years, but she managed to pull herself up. She did it, Nolan. She did. Gotta say, wasn't sorry to see your grandma and grandpa pass."

He saw the sheen of tears in her eyes and gulped. He'd known this woman since he was seven years old. Over twenty years. The only time he'd seen that kind of admiration in her eyes was when he came in to tell her that he'd upped and joined the Navy.

Polly must have seen something in his eyes because her small, veined hand landed on top of his big one. She leaned in. "Nolan you did the right thing leaving all those years ago. Every single one of us cheered you on. It was years before your mama ever got right. Years and years. I truly believe that part of it was because she lost you, and she realized she needed something else to hold onto, something else to find. She found it in herself. I was one of the last people to believe that she'd really changed. But she did, boy."

Her grip was tight as could be, or maybe it was just

that Nolan had lost all of his strength. How was it that after all these years he might have actually had a mother, but he'd thrown it away?

"I've got to go," he muttered.

He got up from the stool and bumped into a couple as he stumbled toward the door. "Sorry," he mumbled.

He made it to his truck and was fumbling with the key fob when somebody shouted his name. He couldn't take it, so he ignored it. He got into the driver's seat and started the car. Someone was knocking on his car window.

"Nolan!"

For a moment he couldn't see past the nose on his face and realized it was the waitress named Kathy. He rolled down his window.

"I'm sorry, I've got to go," he said.

"Hun, here's your food," she said as she shoved two white bags at him, then bent down to pick up a jug of sweet tea. He pulled some twenties out of his wallet.

"Nope. Polly said you're not allowed to pay this time. You can pay the next time. She'd fire my ass if I took your money. Now you go back to that fancy hotel and tell Mary I want the full scoop, and you hug that baby girl for me, you got that?"

Nolan shut his eyes. He was having trouble processing everything.

"Yes, ma'am."

The smell of the food, especially the grits, permeated the cab of the truck. Nolan pressed his head against the headrest, hard. He tried to empty his mind of Polly's words, to rinse out all the images that were flashing in front of his eyes as he smelled the grits on this autumn Tennessee night, but he couldn't.

Now. I need to stay in the now! Think of Mary. Think of Iris.

It wasn't working. When he thought of Iris, he thought of those distinctive blue eyes, and he imagined her red hair in masses of curls, like Mama's.

"Eat all your dinner, Little Man, you want to grow up big and strong."

Her soft hand cupped his cheek as she kissed his forehead.

"I don't like collard greens," he whined.

"You can't have your chocolate brownie iffin you don't eat your collard greens. Just mix it up with your grits, Baby Boy."

"I'm not a Baby Boy," he grinned up at his beautiful mama, "I'm your Little Man."

She laughed and kissed him again.

"That you are. Now eat, son."

Nolan's eyes drifted open. He was trembling, his skin was icy. This was the first time he'd ever had a sweet memory like this with his Mama, ever. It couldn't be true, could it? It was just his mind playing tricks on him.

He looked at his watch.

"Shit."

He had to get a move on.

CHAPTER SIX

Mary heard her phone hum. She always had it on vibrate, never wanting it to disturb Iris. She found it under the baby blanket that she'd spread on the thick carpet near the crib. How it got to be under it, she didn't have the slightest idea.

"Kathy? Why are you calling?"

"It's about Nolan. I wanted to give you a heads-up. Polly talked to him, and he seemed out of sorts."

"Mad?"

"No, muzzy-headed. He forgot to take the food. I had to chase him down and give it to him at his truck."

Mary found that hard to believe. Nolan seemed like one of the most put-together kind of men she'd ever met.

"What'd Polly say to him?"

"I asked, but she wasn't saying. Anyway, you might want to treat him with kid gloves."

"But you're sure he's not angry?" Mary asked again.

The idea of all that muscle being mad sent shivers down her spine.

"He didn't seem to be, but he was sure enough acting weird. Just keep your guard up, okay, girl?"

That's how she'd spent the last six months of her life in Elk Bay around Kyle, keeping her guard up. But in the end, it didn't do her a bit of good. That's how she ended up on the run.

"When did he leave?"

"No more than three minutes ago. I called as soon as I could. But seriously, Hun, I didn't see any mad in that boy. Look, I gotta get back to my customers. Don't be such a stranger. And bring in little miss—we all want to give her some sugar."

"Will do."

Mary plopped down on the pretty sofa, looking down at the cheap burner phone in her hand. She always got a new one in each new place she landed; Brian had taught her that. This was her Jasper Creek phone. Mary wished she could believe that Nolan would be a peaceful man, but she'd heard him say he was a SEAL. She hadn't known that before. SEALs killed people. He must have laughed when she'd threatened him with a gun.

She tried to remember everything that Ginger had told her about her son. She said that he'd gotten into fights at school. She remembered that. Ginger's memory hadn't been all that clear. She said that he might have been bullied, but she wasn't sure.

Mary remembered how Ginger had told her that

when he was fourteen he'd had his growth spurt, and he never came home with any bruises again. It had seemed to Mary that he'd finally been able to defend himself, so bullying was likely the cause of the bruises when he was younger, not him instigating anything. She hoped she was right.

She heard the door opening and looked up. Nolan wasn't smiling, and her gut clenched.

"Are you okay?" she asked tentatively.

"Yeah, why?"

"Your face looks funny."

Darn, I shouldn't have said that.

She needed to keep her mouth shut.

He gave a wan smile. "Just hungry. It's nice we got the suite and it has a table for us to eat at." He deposited the paper bags and the jug of tea on the table and then started distributing the contents.

Mary got up slowly to help, making sure to not make any fast movements.

"How was Iris? Did she wake up?"

"Nope, she slept like a rockstar."

Nolan smiled. "That's good to hear." He opened up their containers and put them out, then placed the plastic utensils and napkins while Mary poured the sweet tea.

"Do you like lemons?"

"I like extra sugar," he said. "I have a sweet tooth," he added with a bit of a grin. And with those words, Mary began to relax.

"Well, let's dig in before Sweet Pea decides it's time for her second dinner." Mary smiled back.

Nolan waited for her to doctor up her sandwich with the extra mayo. As soon as she took a bite of her sandwich and moaned with pleasure, he started digging into his pork chops.

"Now this is living," he groaned. "If I weren't afraid of a heart attack by the time I was forty, I would eat like this every day." His eyes were back to their normal sparkle.

"You're twenty-eight, right?"

"Just turned," he said after he swallowed. "I was born right before Ginger's sixteenth birthday."

Mary forked a good-sized bite of broccoli, promising herself some mac and cheese after she ate all of her broccoli.

"I see you're being a good girl," Nolan said as he pointed his fork toward her pint of vegetables.

"I try. If Slim's cooking I know the fish will be ruined, but the vegetables won't be boiled til they've lost all their flavor, color, and nutrients."

"Sounds like I shouldn't order from Polly's unless I talk to you first," Nolan said.

"Probably not," Mary agreed.

They ate in silence for a bit and Mary relaxed even more. Kathy had been right, Nolan had seemed out of sorts when he'd arrived, but now he was back to normal. She tucked into her sandwich with gusto, enjoying her first real good meal in a couple of days.

She'd missed this. She used to get a full meal every shift she worked at Polly's.

"You're so tiny, where does all that food go?" Nolan asked.

His grin made it clear he was teasing.

"I grew up in a big family. If you didn't grab and eat what you could when you could, you lost out. I learned early to dig in." Mary sat up straighter. "The only one younger than me was Brian, so he and I had to throw elbows to get our portions."

Nolan frowned. "How old was everybody else?"

"I have two older sisters, Ruth and Catherine. They're four and five years older than me. Then there are Peter, Paul, and Matthew; they are twelve, eleven, and nine years older than me."

"Your parents must have sure liked having kids," Nolan commented.

"You'd think so, but it never felt like it."

Mary set down her sandwich and took a big sip of tea.

"It didn't? Why not?"

"It's really complicated, and I don't want to get into it when we have dessert to eat."

"Fair enough."

"Good. We need to get to your ice cream before Iris wakes up and your ice cream melts." She started to open up the smaller containers.

She saw his eyes light up when there were two separate containers for him, one housing the warm apple pie, and another that contained the barely melted vanilla ice cream.

"Voila!" she exclaimed. "I knew Kathy would set you up right."

Mary spooned the vanilla ice cream on top of the warm pie and Nolan took a bite and closed his eyes to savor the flavor.

She watched him with a soft smile as he continued to take bite after bite. He was halfway through his dessert before he put down his fork and looked over at Mary.

"Hey, wait, aren't you going to eat any of your cake?"

"It was more fun watching you enjoy your pie. It was like you were in the middle of a religious experience or something."

"Just a really good memory."

"That's nice." Mary took the first bite of her chocolate cake. She finished a third of hers and put the rest in the hotel's mini-refrigerator. Nolan had demolished his dessert. They'd finished just in time because they heard Iris begin to fuss.

"Can I feed her again?" Nolan asked.

Mary felt her heart melt as easily as his vanilla ice cream. "Absolutely. But only if you learn about diapers."

"I'm ready."

"You only think you are," Mary warned. "This is about the time of night she gifts me with a poopy diaper, so your learning curve is going to be steep."

"I'm a SEAL, bring it on."

"How can you be eating that?" Nolan asked, his voice aghast.

Mary looked down at the chocolate cake she had taken out of the fridge.

"I mean seriously, Mary. How can you? Did you not see and smell what I did?"

"If I let a poopy diaper put me off my food, I'd waste away."

Nolan pretended to shudder. He continued to tease her; it was fun to see if she'd laugh, or throw him sass.

"That wasn't a poopy diaper, that was toxic. They could use that as a weapon of war. Are you sure we don't need to take her to the hospital?"

"The big, bad SEAL taken down by a poopy diaper. I can't wait to tell Trenda. She'll tell her brother and then he'll tell all the other SEALs in the nation. It will be wonderful."

Yep, she was throwing sass. He loved it. She swallowed the last piece of chocolate cake.

"Who's Trenda?"

"She's a friend of mine, and she babysits Iris when I work at Rowdy's. Her brother Drake is a SEAL. I'm not supposed to know he's a SEAL, but her little sister Piper was in town and she let it slip. Trenda got mad at her. Apparently, it's a secret. But since you're both SEALs maybe you know one another?" she asked.

"Normally not, but in this case yes. He's hard to miss. He has a rep."

Mary's eyes got wide. "Not a bad one, I hope? Trenda and Piper are lovely. They love their brother. I was so happy to hear how nice and protective he was toward both of them. He sent them money for years to help them out. He's been an amazing big brother." She started to choke up and turned her face away from him.

"Hey, I didn't mean anything bad. Drake's rep is he is even blunter than I am. He's always putting his foot in it. But most of the time he's pretty damn funny. But there is a running bet to see when he'll be written up by the brass."

She turned back to him, a wobbly smile on her face. "That's good. That makes me happy. I wanted—no needed—to believe that a big brother could be good to his little sisters."

Nolan frowned. "Are you saying that yours aren't?"

He watched her face. A lot of conflicting expressions crossed over it, and finally, she bit her lip, then she opened her mouth.

"I'm not saying my brothers are bad. They were just raised differently. They have a different way of thinking. In their mind, they are doing things that are right and supportive, but to my way of thinking it's bad."

"What have they done?" he asked quietly.

Her lips twisted. "It's a long story that would take

days to explain." She covered her mouth as she yawned. "I'm too tired to get into it."

He knew when to retreat. But something was going on, and he planned to get to the bottom of things.

"It's been a pretty big day, I bet you don't hold a gun on people all that often."

"Thank goodness, not that often."

He frowned. "But you have in the past?"

"Once or twice."

"When? Where?"

"Again, I'm so tired I can barely see straight, and Iris is usually up at around five a.m."

He knew when he'd hit a brick wall. Nolan smiled. "That's perfect, that's about the time I get up too."

"First one up starts the coffee," Mary said around another yawn.

"Deal."

CHAPTER SEVEN

Nolan rolled over and looked at his watch.

"Shit."

He couldn't believe it was seven-thirty in the morning. How in the hell had that happened? He must really have been tired from all that traveling. He really wanted coffee first, but he didn't want to put on clothes before he showered, so he hit the shower. By the time he was done, he smelled both bacon and coffee. How was that possible?

Dragging on a pair of jeans and a t-shirt he meandered into the common room and found Mary lying on the baby blanket, nose-to-nose with Iris. They seemed to be having a staring contest.

"Your food is on the table, as well as a cup of coffee. I stole a bunch of sugar packets when I went down for the free hotel breakfast."

He sat down at the table and found bacon, eggs,

pancakes, and grits. "Thank you so much, Mary, you're a sweetheart."

Nolan started to dig in but continued to watch the two on the blanket. He laughed when Iris took that moment to reach out and pull hard at Maggie's ponytail. "Ouch, you little monster. I told you, no hurting the grown-up, we're fragile." She got face level with Iris and rubbed their noses together. Iris chortled with glee. Nolan watched as the baby then tried to grab Iris's nose.

"Oh, you want to play dirty, huh?" Maggie tapped Iris's nose. "I'm going to get your nose, what do you think about that?"

Nolan heard more joyful baby giggles and he was enchanted. They meshed with Maggie's laughter. Part of him wanted to get down on the floor with her.

What the hell?

He looked down at his breakfast and focused on that, then scrolled through his messages. He grinned when he saw that his teammate Ryker McQueen had reached out to him. Ryker had been like a loose cannon lately. He'd been reaching out to the five members of the team almost weekly, which was so not his M.O.

He finished up what he was eating, then looked over at the blanket one last time. Mary was trying to teach Iris how to sit up, but the little thing was like the Leaning Tower of Pisa—as soon as she was up, she'd lean over, and then she'd fall. But Nolan had to hand it to her, all she'd do was giggle.

"Again?" Mary asked. Iris held out her arms, so Nolan figured that meant yes.

So damned cute.

"Mary, where do we take our plates?"

"I asked when I got breakfast. They said housekeeping would take them when they came to clean later today."

"Gotcha. I'm going to be on the balcony making some calls." She gave him a distracted nod. He watched Iris tip over one last time, loving the sound of her baby giggles.

The weather was perfect outside. Blue skies, green trees, and not a cloud in sight. Nolan took a deep breath. He really had had some good times living here, and he needed to remember that. He sat down on one of the Adirondack chairs, leaned back, and called Ryker. He needed a little bit of amusement.

"Hey," Ryker answered. "How are you doing?"

Nolan frowned. "I'm fine."

"I was so sorry to hear about your mom dying. Is there anything I can do for you? Seriously man, do you need me to fly out? You're in Tennessee, right?"

And that was why he loved his teammate. Ryker might be quite the playboy, with his California surfing good looks, but underneath he had a heart of gold. You could always depend on him.

"Yeah, I'm in Jasper Creek. I just found out about her death a few days ago, but she passed a little over three months ago."

"That's rough. Do you have any other family?"

Nolan craned his neck so he could see Iris through the sliding glass door. He needed to ask Mary who Iris's dad was. Why hadn't he thought of that yesterday?

"Nolan, you still with me?"

"Shit, Ryker, it's all kinds of complicated. I have a little sister that I didn't know about until three days ago. I don't know if her dad's in the picture. I might be all she has."

"Jesus, that's a lot. Who's been taking care of her?"

"That's another thing. I had Gideon do a check on her, and she's somebody who's off the grid. She seems solid. I mean nice and good. But something is totally up with her. She's the one who got in touch with me."

"So I'll repeat my question, do you need me to come out there?"

Nolan laughed to himself when he realized he was considering it. "Nah, I've got this. If all hell breaks loose though, you'll be the first one I'll call. Now you tell me about your girl; isn't her name Amy?"

"Yeah." Just that one word was loaded with dejection. That was so not how Ryker McQueen ever sounded.

"Hey, what's going on? Are you actually serious about a woman? You always said you were going to be exactly like your dad and sow all your wild oats and not marry until you were forty. What's going on?"

"My dad also said that when you find the perfect one, you find the perfect one. I'm not sure, Nolan, but she might be it. God knows that I felt like I had put my finger into a light socket when I first laid eyes on her. She was so vibrant, so funny, and smart. Did you know that she's the lieutenant's fiancée's best friend?"

"I'd heard."

"So you know, she's good people." Ryker laughed. "You should have heard the way Lark warned me off before Amy joined us. Lark's pretty damned funny. She can emasculate you from a hundred yards away. Basically, I was told if I wanted to keep my manly parts I had to keep my hands off Amy."

"So how did you get around Lark? Or Kostya for that matter?" Nolan asked, referring to their lieutenant.

"I smuggled her away to a different hotel bar and took some time to get to know her. We really connected."

This was the most that Nolan had heard about Amy. Yep, Ryker had it bad. "So what's the problem, is it because you live far apart?"

"Nah, D.C. isn't that far from Little Creek. I could make that work. We've been talking on the phone for a couple of weeks. Not long calls, it wasn't like we were teenage girls telling each other our hopes and dreams, but still, they felt good. I was getting to know her. You know?"

Nolan didn't, but he went along. "Sure."

"Then seven weeks ago she stopped taking my calls."

"She blocked you?"

"No, it wasn't that. I could see where she was reading my texts, but she wasn't responding and she wasn't answering my voice mails, or picking up my calls."

"Don't tell me you just let that hang. I know you too well for that."

"Well, I drove to D.C. then went to the restaurant she worked at. Gideon already pointed out how I approached her wrong. She went out the backdoor and I couldn't find her at her apartment. Seriously, she's taken a powder. She's not at her place, and she's asked for time off from her job."

Nolan took a sip of his coffee. "I know you; you're annoying, but not a reason to run away. Something's up."

"That's my take too. But Lark told me to back off for now, that Amy needs her space and Lark has her covered. My hands are tied. It's killing me."

"Yeah, it would me too," Nolan admitted.

"You sure you don't need me to come out to Tennessee? I've never been. We could go to Nashville and become country music stars. How about it?"

Nolan laughed. "Nope. Things are kind of delicate right now, but I can't tell you how much I appreciate it."

"Any time, man. Anytime."

They hung up, then Nolan called Gideon, who had left three calls. It went to voicemail. He wasn't surprised that his lieutenant, Kostya Borona hadn't called; he rarely stuck his nose in any of his men's personal business unless he was worried about their safety.

Next Nolan checked his texts. He had four from Sebastian Durand, two of which were pictures of his nine-month-old son, Neil. The other two just said 'call me' in capital letters. Since Sebastian was out on leave taking care of his wife who had to be on bedrest for her second child, he was out of the loop on what was going on with the team. He must have just found out about Nolan's trip back home.

Nolan was just about to press the button to call his friend when there was a tapping on the sliding glass door. He smiled at Mary who was holding Iris. He motioned for the two of them to join him on the balcony.

"Hey, I want to take Iris for a walk. It's a beautiful day, do you want to come with us?"

He couldn't stop the grin that covered his face. "Absolutely." They'd put her stroller in the bed of his truck, so they had that.

"Okay, I'll go get us bundled up and call down to the front desk and let them know they can clean the room while we're gone."

Nolan nodded as he headed to his room to put on a sweater and boots. One of the amenities that was touted on the Whispering Pines website was that they had a lot of good walking trails in and around their hotel, many of them handicap-accessible, which would be perfect for a stroller. Not that they really needed one—he wouldn't mind carrying Iris.

When he got out into the living room, Mary was putting Iris into a pretty little lavender snowsuit.

"Isn't that overkill?" he asked.

"No, this isn't very thick, but it has this hood that will keep her head warm." As if she knew they were talking about her, Iris started to blow bubbles and wave her arms.

"She's a happy baby, isn't she?" Nolan asked.

"Absolutely. I had to babysit a lot when I was growing up. All babies are different, but I gotta say, and this isn't me being biased, Iris is the easiest and sweetest baby I've ever had to care for."

"Yeah sure," Nolan drawled.

Mary gave him the side eye. "It's the story I'm sticking with."

Iris hadn't taken to Trenda or Bella the way she had latched onto Nolan. It was sweet. Mary wondered if it had been the times that they had stared into one another's eyes. Had Iris seen herself in Nolan and realized on some deep instinctual level that he was a blood relation?

Right now she was pushing an empty stroller while Nolan was holding Iris and pointing out all the different trees and plants to her, telling her their names.

"And that is a hickory tree, Sweet Pea." He held out her hand and tried to get her little finger to point to the tree, but it was a losing battle. He kissed her temple. "Oh look, that there is a chestnut tree. One day we'll get some chestnuts and roast those suckers, and eat them. You'll love it."

Iris pumped herself up and down in his arms.

"Not now, tiger, I saw the damage you could do with just formula. No solid foods for you." Iris chortled.

"Oh, you're laughing are you? Thought it was funny to leave that mess for big brother to clean up, did you?" He kissed her on the cheek.

Mary bit her lip. She felt heat welling up in the back of her eyes, a sure sign that she was wanting to cry, she just didn't know what was getting to her more. Was it the fact that he was referring to himself as big brother, or that he was talking about having a future with Iris? Either way, joy pumped through her veins.

Okay, maybe there's just a little bit of sadness, she admitted as she slowed down. She looked into the empty stroller, letting Nolan walk farther ahead. He'd be so good to Iris. The little girl would always know she was loved if Nolan O'Rourke raised her. Mary's steps slowed even more. The idea of leaving Iris was killing her. Now that it was safe, now that Nolan was here, she could at least admit to herself that part of her had dreamt of staying here and being a mom to Iris, even though she knew that was impossible. But impossible dreams came true sometimes, didn't they?

"Mary? Come on, catch up. Iris is going to test you on the names of the different kinds of trees coming up. If you don't know their names, then she said you have to change her next toxic diaper."

Mary looked up at Nolan's smile and was dazzled.

She still wondered what had happened to him last night at Polly's, but right now, he was just fun to be around.

———

Nolan blew a raspberry on Iris's tummy, but this time he didn't get a giggle, he got a whimper.

"Little girl, you're going to have to tell me what's wrong. You napped, I changed you. I fed you. We played patty-cake. But now you just can't seem to get happy. What's going on?"

He brushed his fingers over her silky tuft of red hair, and she looked up at him with sorrowful blue eyes. She let out a little cry, then started to rub her eyes with her little fists, as a little bubble of snot came out of her nose.

"I don't think you're sick, Sweet Pea, you're not warm." He'd felt her forehead, and her temperature was just fine. The mucus was coming out clear, so no problem there.

He put his clean finger in her mouth and felt around. "Nope, you're not one of those precocious little girls who start teething early, so that's not it." Nolan winked at her, then brushed his nose against the tip of hers.

He had to kind of laugh. Here he was with all this medical training, but he was beginning to freak out when a baby did one of the most natural things that babies did. They cried. They often cried for no apparent reason.

He got up from the floor and put Iris in the crook of his arm. He'd taken to heart what Mary had told him about being relaxed with her, and he made sure that he held her in a relaxed and secure manner. Usually, that hadn't been possible where he'd worked in different parts of the world—the children were either listless or screaming in pain to beat the band.

"Wanna listen to some music?" Nolan asked Iris.

He took out his phone and pulled up his mellowest playlist, which happened to be Christmas music. It had some old classics by Bing Crosby, Frank Sinatra, and Nat King Cole. If he had to spend a lot of time rocking Iris around the suite, at least he could do it to some music.

He was on his twenty-third circuit around the room, and he'd used up all of his small talk when Nat King Cole started singing about chestnuts roasting on an open fire.

"Well, Hallelujah, you stopped crying."

Nolan laughed when she glared at him. And it was a glare, there was no doubting that she wanted him to shut up so she could listen to the song, and he was happy to do it if it would keep her quiet. He should never have told Mary that he had things covered while she went to the library and picked up dinner, what had he been thinking? Just because the last three days had gone so well?

They'd been going *too* well was the problem. Going too well on too many fronts.

Nolan knew damn good and well that Mary was on the run, and he'd given her plenty of openings to let him in. She knew he was a SEAL. She had to know he could help, but she never let out a peep, no matter how many hints he dropped. And boy did he want to help. He'd called Gideon again to see if he could find out anything with the new clues he'd gotten, which wasn't much. She'd mentioned she came from a large family. She'd let drop she was from Minnesota, and she had two older sisters named Catherine and Ruth. But that hadn't been enough for Gideon to find anything.

But the more time Nolan had spent with her, the more desperately he wanted to help her, and it wasn't just because of all she'd done for Iris. It was because of who she was. The woman she was. There was so much to Mary Smith. The woman who had confronted him with a gun, spent almost all of her money on a baby who was no relation to her, and looked mighty fine in yoga pants. So who could blame him for wanting to get her to talk about her past and how he could help her?

But what did she do? She wanted to talk about Ginger.

She'd been nice about it. Gentle, even. But still, she was pushing. It was like she wanted him to get to know Ginger, maybe get a different perspective on her, possibly even get a better opinion about her. What Mary didn't understand was that after talking to Polly, he didn't think he could handle it if his mother had been a person worth knowing and he'd blown his chance to know her.

Iris wiggled in his arms and let out a squeal.

"Oh, was I holding you too tight, or do you not like Dean Martin?"

He bounced with Iris in his arms back over to where his phone was sitting on the coffee table and went back to the Nat King Cole song, and she settled right back down.

"Okay, now that I've got your undivided attention, what do you think of Miss Mary?"

He'd been talking to Iris on and off now for three days, and it no longer felt so weird, but maybe asking for her opinion was a little weird. Of course, as Iris started pumping her arms and legs up and down at the sound of Mary's name, he kind of had his answer.

"You like her, don't you, Sis?"

Nolan reached out and touched one of her tiny hands and she grabbed his finger. "You think you've got me? Is that what you think?"

"Honey, I'm home," Mary cried out as she came in through the front door. "I brought dinner."

Nolan grinned big and looked down to see that Iris's smile was just as big. "We're both hooked, aren't we, Sweet Pea?"

CHAPTER EIGHT

"Christmas music?" Mary frowned when she came through the door holding the bags from Polly's.

"It's a long story, but Iris is partial to Nat King Cole."

"Who?" Mary asked as she tore open the bags and set out all of the goodies on the table. It felt good to get out some of her aggression.

"You know, the guy from the fifties who sang 'The Christmas Song'. That's the one that starts, 'Chestnuts roasting on an open fire, Jack Frost nipping at your nose.'"

"Yeah, I know that song, I just didn't know who sings it. Slim wasn't cooking this evening, so you're getting catfish. You have a really nice singing voice. I hope I did the right thing getting you the catfish, you sounded like you wanted it the other night. This time instead of grits I got you okra. I hope that's okay."

"Hey, are you okay?"

Shoot, she'd been talking a mile a minute. She did that when she was stressed and Nolan noticed. Time to get herself together.

"I'm fine. Just hungry is all."

"Well it smells great, thank you," Nolan said. He walked over with Iris in the crook of his arm. Mary looked down at her. Her eyelids were drooping, she'd be asleep soon. "I was surprised when she didn't like Luke Bryan."

"Huh?" Mary was confused, she couldn't follow what he was saying. Everything was falling apart around her ears, so Nolan talking about nonsense wasn't helping. Maybe if she mentioned his apple pie he would stop. "I got you apple pie again."

Nolan went over to the coffee table and picked up his phone that was still playing music. He thumbed through something. "This is Luke Bryan, you know, the country music artist. I played his rendition of 'O Holy Night'. She didn't like it."

Iris gave a snuffling sound.

"Well, don't play it. We don't want her to wake up. Here, give her to me and I'll put her down in her crib. You start eating before your food gets cold."

She took the baby from Nolan and went into her bedroom where the crib was. She gently placed Iris on her back, just like all the books had told her, and Iris immediately rolled over onto her stomach and put her thumb into her mouth.

Mary's breath hitched.

"It's going to kill me to leave you, baby girl. I

wanted to be your Mama so bad. But he'll hurt you. He always hurts the things I love."

Somehow Mary managed not to break down into sobs. She couldn't wake Iris, and she couldn't alert Nolan that there was trouble. She needed a plan. She couldn't just run without a plan—that was how Kyle almost caught her that first time.

I need a plan!

Her expression calm, she went out to the common area and saw that Nolan had plated their food. He was playing some other music, not a Christmas song.

She went over to the mini refrigerator and got out the jug of sweet tea from the day before. She also pulled out one of her precious cans of Orange Crush soda pop that she'd purchased when she'd made a quick grocery store run. Now that was like being at home in Minnesota; they hardly ever got this pop at home, but when they did, it was a real treat.

"That's pretty. I like that," she said, pointing to his phone as she sat down at the table.

"What kind of music do you like? Country? Pop? R&B? Heavy Metal? Classics?"

Mary sat down, then concentrated on putting extra mayo on her turkey and cranberry sandwich and opening her can of Orange Crush.

"I don't know. I guess I like what you're playing."

"So you like R&B."

Mary shrugged. "I guess so. The only time I really hear music is when I'm working at Rowdy's, but then the music is so loud it's just noise that makes it hard for me to hear people when I'm trying to take their drink orders."

"So what do you listen to in the car?"

"Podcasts and audiobooks." She took a sip of her drink, trying to stop his line of questioning.

"I don't know how you can drink that, it's like drinking syrup," Nolan teased.

"Well, after all the sugar you put into your sweet tea, I'll say the same thing back to you."

"What's the latest audiobook you've read?" he asked.

"The Art of Power," Mary answered after she swallowed her bite of sandwich. "I think you'd like it."

"Why?"

Mary looked at him and saw that Nolan looked truly interested, so she would give him her real answer, which she didn't often do. Hopefully, if they talked about that, he'd quit asking her other questions.

"It was a biography of Thomas Jefferson. He was complex, like you."

Nolan snorted. "I'm not complex, what you see is what you get."

"Yeah, sure. You told me all the extra training you did so you could become a medic. You said you even worked with babies when you were in other countries, but there you were, terrified with your baby sister to begin with."

"That's one thing."

"How about the part where you won't talk about

your mom, but I see how close you are with your team, so I know you're not a loner."

Shoot, she could see she was making him uncomfortable, but at least they were talking about him, and not her.

"My history with Ginger is complicated. You're still not telling me how you figure I'm like somebody so great as Thomas Jefferson."

"He was often in conflict with himself. Ultimately, he followed his conscience to do the right thing, even when he desperately wanted and sometimes did the wrong thing."

"What do you mean? I don't get it."

"He could be a good friend, but a vengeful enemy. That goes against his principles. Then there was the way he treated the mother of his children. It's odd that a culture that happened almost two hundred and fifty years ago is how I was raised..." Her voice drifted off.

She thought about her dad, and how he tried to force her into marrying Kyle, even though he had proven himself to be abusive as a child and an adult. When she thought back to when he killed that cat in front of her and Brian...

"Mary?" Nolan touched her forearm. "Are you with me?"

She shook her head and tried to smile but failed. She set down her sandwich. "Oh yeah, I was telling you why I thought you would like the book, or rather I thought the book would be good for you. It's been good for me. It makes you realize that not everything is black and white. I mean, some things definitely are." She shuddered. "Some things are evil. But sometimes things are gray."

Nolan picked up her hand and slid his fingers between hers, their meals forgotten. "What's evil?"

"Nothing," she shook her head so hard that the rubber band holding her hair in its ponytail broke and her long hair spilled all around her. She pushed her chair back from the table, worried she might have mayo or cranberries in her hair.

Nolan sighed and pushed her food away from the edge of the table. "What's evil?" he asked again.

This time she just shook her head.

———

Nolan pushed his half-eaten meal aside then got up and went over to the couch. "Come sit next to me," he suggested. Okay, he tried to make it sound like a suggestion, but it came out more like an order. At least she complied.

She sat against the far corner, her feet on the cushions, her knees up under her chin, her arms holding them there. Yep, totally a defensive posture. He scooched closer, not enough so they were touching but close enough to share body heat. And she needed it—she was shuddering again.

"You've got to tell me why you're running."

She shook her hair again so that part of it ended up falling across her face. He knew she wanted to hide behind it, but he wasn't going to allow it. He tucked it behind her ear and she gave him the same kind of glare that he'd thought Iris had.

"Talk to me, Mary."

"I'll tell you what, if you'll listen to me about Ginger, I'll talk to you about me." He opened his mouth, but she held up a finger. "With an open mind. You have to listen about your mom with an open mind. That's the deal."

Nolan lowered his head. He knew this was coming. Ever since Polly had told him that his mother had made major life changes, he *knew* this was coming.

He nodded his head. "But you have to go first."

"Hey, it's not going to be bad. It's going to be good, I promise you," Mary said in a reassuring tone.

"Again, you have to go first."

"Okay. But it's complicated."

"Complicated is my job, Honey."

She smirked. "That's another thing you and Thomas Jefferson have in common, you both believe you can handle anything."

He reached out and touched her hand. She grasped it, reminding him of Iris. "Talk to me, Honey."

She blew out a long breath.

"I have to start out about where I was raised. How I was raised. My father is the head of our household. What he says goes. Absolutely. When my two sisters turned eighteen and nineteen, in his mind it was time for them to marry. Elk Bay is a small community, so there weren't a lot of boys their age to choose from, but that didn't matter. There were still a lot of men who were interested in younger wives."

"Like a cult?" Nolan asked carefully.

"No, we're not a cult," Mary quickly defended. "We don't have a leader, but there is a ruling council. It goes back to the eighteen-hundreds."

Nolan tried to wrap his head around what she was saying.

"So like the Amish?"

"No, not like that. We believe in taking advantage of modern technology, at least for the men. It's the women who can't drive, or have phones or use computers. We're basically owned by our fathers, and if they die, we're then owned by our older brothers, or younger brothers if there aren't older brothers. I have three older brothers. They're twelve, eleven, and nine years older than me. Their names are Peter, Paul, and Mathew. I mentioned my older sisters before, didn't I?"

"Catherine and Ruth. How much older are they than you?"

"Catherine is four years older, and Ruth is five years older. They both got married six years ago. Because there weren't boys their age, my father arranged marriages with older men. Ruth married Mr. Stephens; he was a widower with three daughters. He was—I mean is, well was at the time—about fifty years old. At least Catherine's husband was just forty."

Nolan couldn't believe what he was hearing. "Didn't they have a choice? How old were your sisters at the time? How old are you?"

"I'm twenty-one. My sisters were nineteen and eighteen. The only reason Father was waiting to marry me to Kyle is because he was going to college in International Falls. I was supposedly lucky because he was young like me."

"Did they have any say as to who they had to marry? Did you?"

She looked down at her knees but squeezed his hand so hard that if she were a man she'd be crunching his bones.

"No, we're women, we don't get choices."

"What are some of the other laws? And how can this exist in America?" Nolan asked, trying to understand the whole picture.

"Elk Bay is truly isolated. We're fifty miles from the nearest city, and that's the Canadian city of Thunder Bay. That's where we go to get supplies. Since we don't mix with other Americans, nobody really knows about us, and if they did, they'd probably just stay clear."

"I'm assuming you're home-schooled?"

"The boys through high school. A very few are selected to go to college in International Falls."

Nolan rubbed the back of his neck. Her story seemed like something out of a movie. A bad movie. "You said the boys, what about the girls?"

"We had to stop school at thirteen, then we had to learn how to keep a house so that we could become a good wife."

"Okay, but I don't understand, how could you have lived like that for so long, and be so articulate?"

"You think I'm articulate?" Mary looked up at him for the first time and gave a shy smile.

"Damned right I do. If you hadn't told me all of this, I would have thought you came from a normal background. I mean, I would have thought you had at least completed high school."

This time she smiled big. "Thank you. But I owe a lot of it to my younger brother Brian. He snuck me the books and made sure I could get onto the computers. Well, he's my younger brother by two minutes. We're twins. We couldn't really act like there was a special relationship or anything, because there was such a line between men and women, but we looked out for one another."

"What made you run away, besides the fact that it was a shitty environment? Was it because they were forcing you into a marriage?"

Mary nodded. "The boy I was engaged to, he was... All of my siblings, except for Brian, thought I was so lucky because I was being engaged to someone my own age. We were both nineteen, and I was long in the tooth. But they were waiting for Kyle to come home from college."

"He couldn't have finished college unless he started really early."

"He told everybody that he finished, but Brian checked up on him. He lied. He'd been kicked out, but his father would never believe that his son would ever lie."

"So Kyle is who you're running from?"

Mary nodded her head. Her anguish was clear and so was her fear. "Mary, why are you so scared of him?"

"He's a psychopath. I didn't know that word before I left Elk Bay, Brian and I just knew he was evil. We'd seen him kill small animals when we were growing up. When I was sixteen, we knew that we were going to be matched. I didn't want him. He scared me. He was a bully. He told me he would kill our family dog if I didn't do whatever he wanted. I knew he wouldn't. King was a pitbull, there was no way he could kill him. But a month later King was dead. Hit by a car. I knew Kyle did it."

Nolan's blood ran cold.

"Kyle said Catherine's little boy would be next if I didn't say yes to our match. I believed him. I said yes."

"How old were you when you ran away?"

"Eighteen the first time. Mama was arranging the wedding. I knew that once I was married to him, he'd end up killing me or our children. I had to get away."

Nolan couldn't begin to imagine what her married life would have been like if she'd actually married the psycho.

"I told Mama that I wanted to pick out the material for my dress, so she took me to Canada, and that was when I made a break for it. I'd taken some of the family money, I didn't have a choice."

Her voice was hoarse with tears.

"Honey, you had to do what you had to do. I'm proud of you."

"Brian had told me about a motel that needed a

maid, and he said that they paid in cash and I would get a room. I took a bus to get there. After a week, Kyle found me." Her hoarse voice had turned into a mere whisper.

"What happened when he found you?"

Nolan pleaded to heaven that he hadn't raped her.

"He said he had to drag me back home, but first I needed to know who I belonged to from now on. He hit me in the face once, then after that, he concentrated on hitting me where nobody would notice, then he tied me down and duct-taped my mouth shut. He had a big hunting knife that he used on me. When I woke up in the motel, there was blood everywhere. I was still kind of bleeding. He threw bandages at me and told me to get myself cleaned up so we could get home. It wasn't until I was cleaning up that I saw he'd cut his initial into my body."

Nolan looked at the tiny woman in front of him and tried to imagine what had happened. When he did, he thought he would throw up. Mary didn't seem to notice his reaction. She was crying.

"Can I hold you?" he asked quietly.

She looked up at him and reached out with her other hand and he caught it. Slowly she let down her legs and curled them under herself, then shifted her body so that her head and torso were leaning against him. He lifted their clasped hands and drew her into the circle of his arms. She snuggled closer.

"I see you with Iris, you know," she whispered.

It took him a minute to process what she meant by

that. Then he realized that she trusted him because of how careful he was with his baby sister.

"I would never, ever hurt you. I would only want to make you feel good."

Shit, had he said that? Yep, he had. And he meant it too.

"You do, Nolan. You make me feel safe. I don't think I've ever felt so safe. At least for this moment in time."

Nolan instantly went on alert. "You are safe. You'll always be safe with me. That's what I do, Honey. I keep people safe."

She didn't respond, she just cuddled closer.

Nolan figured that for now, he'd just have to live with this uncertainty. He'd probe more later. He was just happy she'd shared this much.

"Is Mary your real name?" he asked.

She shook her head.

"I didn't think so, but it's a good thing you dyed your blond hair red; it changed your appearance quite a bit."

She sighed, her warm breath heating his neck. "It did. I'll have to touch up my roots."

"Would you be willing to tell me your real name?"

She moved her head from its resting place and gave him a long assessing look.

"Your first name?" Damn, he sounded like he was pleading, and maybe he was.

"Margaret," she whispered. "Everybody calls me Maggie."

"That's a pretty name. When it's just the two of us can I call you Maggie?"

She blew out a long breath. "I'd like that. I call myself Auntie Maggie to Iris all the time."

"She has been blessed to have you," he said sincerely.

Tears gathered in her eyes. "Do you really think that?"

"Absolutely."

CHAPTER NINE

Maggie put on another coat of eyeliner. It was always so dark at Rowdy's and she always got so much guff from Kurt that she wasn't wearing enough make-up, that she now just slathered it on. She stepped back from the mirror and took another look.

"Better."

She knew that Nolan was out there waiting, and she still wasn't quite ready for him to see her in this get-up, so she picked up the mascara. The problem was that stupid conversation she'd had with him on the couch yesterday. It had been a turning point in how Maggie looked at Nolan, and it scared her. It scared her a lot. She needed to be leaving soon, that's why she needed this weekend and next weekend at Rowdy's to top off her emergency fund. Instead, she was thinking of Nolan in an entirely inappropriate way.

There had only been one man that she'd shared

kisses with in her entire life, and that was Jake Sanders. He'd been the owner of the dude ranch where she had worked in Arizona. It was the second to the last place she'd hidden before coming to Tennessee.

When Mary had successfully run away the second time it was because Brian had arranged everything down to the nth degree, and it had worked. He'd purchased three bus tickets—two she didn't use, the third one went to Idaho. He made her dye her hair before she got onto the bus. He had given her twelve hundred dollars in cash that time, and he had a friend waiting for her in Idaho.

Carla had been a godsend. She explained how to get the burner phone, how to access the new e-mail account that Brian had set up, and she let Maggie sleep on her couch for two months before she helped her find a job in Arizona. The best thing that Carla had done for her was to teach her how to drive!

Maggie was heartbroken when she had to leave Carla, but exhilarated about her next adventure. She was finally going to live free! When she got to Wickenburg, Arizona she couldn't believe how welcoming everybody was, especially the owner, Jake Sanders. She got to work as the cook at the dude ranch, and it took her a week to get into the swing of things. But she figured it out. She spent four and a half months there. Jake was a special man, his dad had died early in life and left the ranch to Jake, and he was making a go of things. It took months for Maggie to figure out that he was interested in her in a romantic way.

Jake coaxed her out of her shell, and she would have stayed longer, except Jake developed deep feelings for her. She couldn't abide by the fact that she might be leading him on, so she set out to her next stop.

The day Nolan arrived was when she logged onto her private e-mail address after her WeChat with Brian. She'd wanted to see if Carla had any news. When she logged in, instead of e-mails from either Brian or Carla, there was a new sender, and there was an attachment. It was titled Jake Sanders, so she *had* to open it.

It was a long article in the Arizona newspaper that explained how Jake had been in a bad automobile accident when the brake line to his truck had been cut, and the brake fluid leaked out. He was lucky he didn't die. The local sheriff's department was following up on all leads in the case, and Jake was still hospitalized.

That was it. It came from a Gmail account that was nothing but numbers. There was nothing else written, just that attached article. Maggie immediately got online and looked for any updates on Jake's status and couldn't find any. She couldn't figure out how to find out how he was doing without Kyle being able to trace it back to her, here in Jasper Creek, which she knew he wanted.

The last time she'd seen Jake had been eighteen months ago.

How could I have brought that on Jake?

I need to warn Nolan.

I need to leave.

Now.

But how could she until she had Nolan's promise that he would take in Iris to raise?

She blew out a deep breath, then another, then another.

She stepped back four paces from the mirror and gave herself one last look and sighed. She hated the Rowdy's uniform; it made her so uncomfortable. The only good thing was that Kurt had let her skip the stilettos when he'd seen how poorly she'd walked in them. Instead, she was just wearing a two-inch heel, which was bad enough in her opinion.

She walked out into the common area where Trenda Avery, her daughter Bella, and Nolan were waiting.

"You know, you really don't have to come to the bar with me, Nolan,"" she said for the fourth time.

He didn't say anything, just looked at her hair that she'd blow-dried into thick waves, her black camisole top that pushed her breasts up high and out there for everyone to see, the red miniskirt, and fishnet stockings. He finally said something something. "I'm going to the bar."

Trenda chuckled and chuckled. "I sure didn't see that coming...not."

Her precocious little black-haired daughter tugged at her mother's hand. "Why are you laughing?"

"No reason, Lovebug," she brushed back her daughter's black curls and smiled. "No reason."

Bella turned to Maggie. "You look beautiful. I'm

going to wear clothes just like that when I grow up. Can you put some of your red lipstick on me?"

"Fuck no," Nolan growled.

Maggie's eyes got big. She was shocked that Nolan had said the 'F' word in front of the child. Bella turned around to look at the big man and held out her hand. "You owe me a dollar."

Nolan frowned for a moment, then turned to Trenda and said, "Drake, right?"

Trenda nodded.

Bella piped up. "Uncle Drake gives me a dollar per swear word. Sometimes he puts some on account. Last time he had a lot of friends over, so he gave me a fifty-dollar bill. Are you going to swear a lot?"

Nolan pulled out his wallet and shuffled through his bills. Maggie was pretty sure he couldn't find any dollar bills. He pulled out a five. "Okay, I get four more swear words," he said as he placed the bill in her small hand.

"Nice doing business with you, Mr. O'Rourke."

"Since you're fleecing me, call me Nolan."

Bella grinned bigger. "Okay, Nolan. Are you a SEAL like Uncle Drake?"

Maggie watched as he rubbed the back of his neck. "First, there is nobody like your uncle Drake, but yeah, I'm a SEAL."

"Good, you can take care of Mary. Sometimes she comes back to our house and whispers to Mom. She's really mad. Once she came home and her hair was wet, and she smelled funny. That time she was crying."

Maggie wanted the floor to open up so she could be swallowed up—she didn't want to hear any of Nolan's guff. She'd been telling Nolan how nice and calm Rowdy's was, and now she'd been outed by a six-year-old!

"Don't worry, Bella, I'll take care of things."

"I'm going to be late, we'd better go," she said to Nolan. She turned to Trenda. "Do you have everything?"

Trenda hefted up the bag she always carried to show Maggie. Maggie knew that it contained everything she needed to keep Bella entertained, plus all of the child's school books to do her homework.

"Are you sure we shouldn't have dropped Iris at your house?" Maggie asked for the millionth time.

"No, please, Mom, no. I want to stay here. It's cool. Plus the TV is so big, and I can tell all my friends I got to stay the night at the Whispering Pines. Please, Mom?"

Trenda looked at Bella, then looked back up at Maggie and shrugged.

"Gotcha," Maggie smiled.

"You ready?" Nolan asked.

Maggie nodded.

"Where's your coat?"

She pointed to the sweater that was slung over the back of the couch.

"Dammit, Maggie... I mean Mary, that's not a coat. It's cold out there." He took off his leather jacket and threaded her arms through the sleeves. He then rolled up the sleeves and zipped it up. As he turned back for the door, Maggie caught sight of his gun before he untucked his shirt, and then it was gone.

"Let's go."

"You only have three swears left," Bella called out as they exited the hotel.

Shit, shit, shit!

The yoga pants were bad enough, but this outfit? *No bueno!*

And what was this shit about her being covered in beer and crying? Just what kind of shit did this guy Kurt let happen over at Rowdy's? Nolan intended to have a talk with him. First, he was going to get a lay of the land, then he'd have a serious talk.

Also, what kind of perfume was she wearing? He'd never smelled it before. It was driving him crazy.

"Let me help you into the truck," Nolan said as he opened the passenger door.

"You always say that, but I'm perfectly capable of doing this myself."

"Humor me."

Maggie sighed and extended her hand, but Nolan saw her little smile. He went to his side, buckled up, and got them on the road. Holy hell, he was totally surrounded by that damned perfume, and it was delicious.

"You wear perfume when you go to the bar?"

"Of course not," Maggie protested.

"Yes, you are. I've been living with you for four days now, and this is the first time you've smelled like peaches."

"Oh, that's just my lotion. The camisole chafes my... Well, it chafes, so I use lotion and powder and it helps."

Fuck me. Now I'm going to be thinking of her peach-smelling breasts, and how her ass looks like the ripest peach I've ever seen!

"Do you have to wear this outfit?"

"It's my uniform. If I don't wear it, I don't work there. At least I don't have to wear the stilettos."

Fucking Christ! Stilettos? I'd lose my mind!

"Yeah, I guess that's a blessing. Now tell me what would send you home crying or make you mad."

"Oh, it's nothing."

"No, it's something. So, tell me."

"Sometimes the customers get a little out of hand, but I handle it." She gave a half-hearted laugh. "Did you hear that? 'Out of hand', 'handle'? Kind of funny, right?"

"Not in the slightest, Darlin'." Nolan's accent was really thick. "Don't they have bouncers at this place?"

"Sure they do, but that's only for the real bad stuff. I mean when they try to rip off your uniform or something like that."

Nolan couldn't even respond to that. He had no words. He turned on his blinker, then merged onto the highway. After he was safely on the highway he took a quick glance over at Maggie. "Please tell me that is *not* the threshold for the bouncers to get involved," he said softly.

"Uhm, yeah," she answered, like she was telling him the weather.

"So tell me, Maggie, what are the customers allowed to do?"

She turned around in the truck's seat and looked at him. "Nothing. I mean when someone tries to grab my breast, or tries to put his hand up my skirt, of course I tell him no and push him away. That's what we're supposed to do."

"But you don't call a bouncer over?"

"No, because that's not something they want to kick a customer out for. Fighting and something close to assault I guess is what the parameters are for the bouncers. Kurt says that's why the pay's so good. He says we know the rules and we choose to work there, and he's right."

"Oh, he does, does he?"

"Yeah."

"Have you ever worked in a bar before?" Nolan asked.

"No. But you've got to remember, I don't have papers, so I can't work most places. I need to work and be paid in cash only."

"Why don't you have papers?" Nolan asked.

"Brian couldn't find any of our birth certificates.

But most of us were home births, so there probably weren't any, and we read online that without a birth certificate we couldn't get a driver's license or a social security card."

"Rowdy's is whacked. If the authorities got wind of what they're doing, they'd be shut down in a New York minute. At the very least they'd lose their liquor license."

"I know they don't want that. I have to card anybody who doesn't look twenty-one. But Kurt says if they're underage and have a fake ID it's okay to serve them because he won't be liable."

"Hmmm."

"You say that a lot."

"You tell me a lot of things where that's the only appropriate response."

"Nolan, don't ruin this for me, okay? Rent is due next week, and I won't be able to pay it without working this full weekend and next weekend."

"Let me give you the money. After all, I owe you for all you've done for Iris."

"I don't want your money."

"I told you, I owe it to you for having taken care of Iris."

"I won't take it. Taking care of Iris has been a joy for me. Back in Elk Bay, I got to take care of a lot of the babies and young children. I've been missing them. That's one of the things that hurts the most, knowing I'll never get married and have a family of my own. So no, I won't take a dime for doing something that's been so much of a pleasure for me."

"Why won't you have a family of your own?"

"I'm afraid of what it will be like. I just don't see how it will be good. I think eventually it will turn out bad for me."

Nolan thought about some of his teammates' marriages.

"Maggie, you realize that most of the world isn't like Elk Bay, don't you?"

"Yes. Maybe," she said slowly. "But I saw what happened, especially to Paul, my brother. He was so nice and good before he went off to college and came back. Then he became just like Father. He treats Willow, the woman he married, just like Father treats Mama. Paul used to really like Willow and was nice to her once, but now he's cold and dictatorial. He changed. I'm afraid to risk it."

"Do you think that would happen to your brother Brian?" Nolan asked reasonably.

"I really, really hope not. He has this girl he's sweet on in Elk Bay. She is so wonderful, I just can't imagine him acting like Paul. But then again, he plans to take Laurel away. So that could make a difference."

"There you go then, it's Elk Bay. Talk to Trenda—she'll tell you about good marriages, they're out there."

"I haven't wanted to because I know there is something that might not be so good from her past. She's never mentioned Bella's father, and I didn't want to stir up any bad memories."

"I'm pretty sure her brother is married. Ask about that."

He took the exit that would take them to Rowdy's, and his gut clenched. The next few hours were not going to be good.

"That's a good idea, I'll ask her."

CHAPTER TEN

Maggie could feel Nolan's eyes on her, even though he was sitting far away with his back to the wall. He was nursing his third beer, but she knew that he hadn't really finished the first two, he was just spending money so he wouldn't be kicked out.

It was only nine o'clock, so everyone was well behaved so far. The new girl, Heather had had a problem over near the pool tables, but before she had a chance to wade in, she saw that another one of the more experienced waitresses had stepped in. Maggie hated having to serve near the pool tables; the men could turn ugly if they were losing, and sometimes they could get disgusting with how they would touch the waitresses with their pool cues. Luckily, she was serving underneath the TV near the front of the house tonight.

By ten o'clock things were beginning to pick up and

that was when Kurt came over and tapped her on the shoulder.

"Need you to work the pool area. Had to fire the new girl."

Maggie turned around and looked up at the beefy bar manager. "You told me that with the reduced shifts I wouldn't have to work the pool area."

"I said that I was doing you a favor giving you reduced shifts and you'd do whatever I fucking needed you to do. Now do you need this job or not?"

How he could talk with such a big wad of tobacco in his mouth, Maggie had no idea. She watched in disgust as a little bit of tobacco drool dripped out the corner of his mouth.

Maggie nodded.

"Good, get your uppity ass over there now. I'll have Phyllis take over this area."

Maggie wound her way through the tables and rounded the bar. She grabbed a tray so she could bus tables when she got to the back area where the eight pool tables were set up. It was crowded and she could feel the tension in the air. On three of the high tops, there were a lot of empty shot glasses, which didn't bode well, and on two of the pool tables, she saw hundred-dollar bills being bet. These were not indicators of a casual evening. What was worse, there was not one single couple in the back to mellow things out.

She continued to survey the room and finally spotted two men she recognized. Titus Rutherford and

Arlo something-or-other. They were bad news. Titus
ran the bank in Jasper Creek, and Arlo was his little
flunky. No matter what Titus ever did, Kurt never
kicked him out. Titus had been making hard passes at
her almost since the day she started here. He'd been
getting handsy, but nothing too overt. No, he was the
type who had to try to 'buy' his way into her affections.
He made her feel filthy.

Don't make eye contact.

She started on the left side of the room.

"What can I get for you?" she asked the three men
who were obviously waiting for a pool table to open up.

"Bud," the first one answered.

"Coors," the big blond said.

"Make it two Buds," the smaller blond said.

Maggie nodded, then cleared their table and put
the empties onto her tray. She went down the line to
the next two tables before going to the bar and putting
in her order. Maggie then started on the fourth table
when she went back.

"What the fuck?! Are you just going to ignore us?
We're here too." She looked over her shoulder and saw
a clearly drunk man in a cut-off t-shirt with a trucker's
hat holding up an empty beer glass.

"Which one is your table, sir?" Maggie asked just
loud enough so he could hear. She didn't want to sound
like she was yelling because that would just upset
the man.

"I don't remember," he yelled. "But my beer is
empty. Come take my glass and my order."

Maggie looked at the four occupants of table four, which was covered with empty shot glasses and lime wedges.

Great, tequila. Yeah, sure, they're going to be patient.

"Let me take these gentlemen's order, then I'll get your order and take it to the bar, how does that sound?"

"I want a beer now," he yelled.

Maggie breathed a huge sigh of relief when the person he was playing pool with insisted he take his shot. She turned to the four men and smiled.

"What can I get for you?"

"She said, you, not y'all. You're a Yankee, right?" The whipcord-lean man with gray hair asked.

"Who cares where she's from, look at those tits." This came from the man with a huge belly.

"Your orders?" Maggie asked as she reached out and started clearing their table.

"Are you on the menu?"

Like I haven't heard that line a million times, you big jerk.

"I can come back if you're not ready to order."

She grabbed the last shot glass, ready to step back and go to the next table, when pot-belly grabbed her wrist.

Darn it!

"Don't walk away from us. You're our waitress. Your job is to serve us," he said.

"Nah, her job is to *service* us," the lean guy with gray hair said.

Maggie twisted her wrist, trying to break his grip

but it was tough, and she had a problem since she was also trying to balance the tray with her other hand.

"Gentlemen," she gave a smile and looked each man in the eye. "I will call a bouncer over, and then your night out will be over. Is that really how you want things to end?" She was bluffing, but they didn't have to know it.

"Oh really? I don't see a bouncer," Pot-belly said.

"Look up at the ceiling, in the corner. See that camera? All I have to do is give the high sign," Maggie lied.

Pot-belly let go of her wrist.

"Thank you, now may I take your order?"

One of the four who hadn't had anything to say so far asked for a round of double shots of Patron tequila.

Great, they're getting drunk at twice the rate. I'll just deliver them slow.

"Are you done flirting over there? I want my beer!"

Maggie turned around and went to Trucker Hat, got his beer order, and took his empty glass. That was when she noticed Nolan walking up to the edge of the pool room, then taking a spot to lounge against the wall since there were no empty tables. He was carrying one of his half-finished beers. She couldn't decide if she was happy about his presence or not, but she didn't have time to think about it, she had orders to fill.

At the bar, she talked to Adam the bartender. He had her first order waiting for her, but she asked for the shots and the new beer order too, knowing she'd have trouble on her hands if she didn't bring *all* the orders at the same time.

Maggie was relieved when she didn't have any problems serving the drinks. She handed out bills where necessary and kept track of who still had a tab going. She moved to table five then had to go to the dreaded table six. Titus had nine one-hundred-dollar bills placed out in front of him on the small high-top table. Not fanned, no, they were placed, so there was no mistaking that there were nine bills.

"Hi there, Sweet Cheeks. So glad you came over here to work tonight," Titus said in his used car salesman voice.

Maggie looked at a spot over his shoulder and smiled. "Hello. What would you like to drink tonight?"

Arlo snickered.

She hated that little man. He was so sneaky. Shannon and Phyllis had told her bad stories about him. Both of them had gone to high school with Titus and Arlo. Apparently, there used to be a third guy, but he was in prison now.

"Mary, tell me what I can buy with nine hundred dollars. Isn't that enough to cover your rent for the month?" Titus asked.

How did he know that?

"I'd like to take your drink order. If you don't have one, I'll move to the next table."

Arlo laughed again. He sounded like a braying donkey.

"You didn't answer my question," Titus said gently.

Maggie turned her head and looked Titus in the eye, and spoke just as gently. "You didn't answer my question, sir. What would you like to drink? Perhaps I should phrase that differently. Here in a bar, people normally request a beverage with alcohol in it. Would you like me to get you one of those...sir?"

He squinted at her. "Our little Mary is trying to be funny. Did you hear that, Arlo?"

This time Arlo giggled and it sounded like nails on a chalkboard. Mary winced.

"I think we need to take this talk to Kurt's office, don't you Arlo?"

"Yeah, Titus. That's a good idea."

What a little toad.

"And what makes you think I'll go anywhere with you?"

"Because you don't want people to know you've been living in that shitty little trailer with that slut Ginger's brat. And you really don't want me to tell my buddy at CPS how hazardous that place is and how you've been endangering her all this time."

Maggie felt cold sweat dripping down her spine.

"If you don't do exactly what I want, right now, I'll have that baby ripped out of your arms and put in foster care so fast, it'll make your head spin."

CHAPTER ELEVEN

They were across the room. One of them had his back to him and Maggie was in front of the other, but Nolan would bet his bottom dollar that they were Titus Rutherford and Arlo Jackson. What were the chances of that happening?

So far they hadn't put their hands on her, but it was taking far too long for her to take their drink orders. He would give it two more minutes, then he'd mosey on over.

Titus—and it was Titus—was picking something up from the table. Then Nolan watched in horror as he stuffed whatever it was down the front of Maggie's camisole. She was frozen stiff but she did nothing to stop him.

What the hell?

Arlo and Titus got up off their chairs and Titus put his arm around Maggie's shoulders, then Arlo was on her other side as they made their way out of the pool room. When Maggie spotted him, she mouthed the word 'help' and he gave her an infinitesimal head nod. He let them pass, then after they were far enough forward, he began to stalk his prey.

He watched as the three of them walked up to the man who had spoken to Maggie before she'd changed locations to work. Nolan assumed that was Kurt the manager. Kurt handed a set of keys to Titus and smiled, then walked right past Nolan as he moved toward the front of the bar.

He'd get to Kurt later. First, he needed to find out what in the hell was going on. Why was Maggie going with them? There was definitely something wrong, and he was going to find out what. What's more, there was no way he was going to let Titus and or Arlo spend one second alone with Maggie.

He followed the trio until they got to a door that was painted the same black as the back wall panel. Most people wouldn't even realize that it was a door. Titus inserted the key and shoved Maggie in front of him. Nolan was closer now, and before the door had a chance to close, he grabbed it. When he opened it, he saw that it led down a hallway. At the end of the hallway was an emergency exit, and Nolan didn't want them to escape through there. The three of them were huddled near another door, and Titus was fumbling through the keys.

Why isn't Maggie struggling, now? What in the hell is going on?

Nolan waited until they had the door open, then he

sprinted down the hall and squeezed in right before it closed.

"Who the fuck are you?" Arlo demanded in a high-pitched whine.

Titus didn't say anything, he just kept his arm around Maggie and studied Nolan.

The last time Nolan had seen Titus was when they were about sixteen. They'd both had their growth spurts by then and were about the same height. Titus was playing football, so he was building a lot more muscle mass than Nolan, but Nolan had learned to fight dirty at some of the foster homes he'd lived in, so he hadn't been worried about Titus. Anyway, Titus was too busy being Homecoming king and football captain to give a shit about Nolan, but when he did see him, he never failed to call him No-Good.

"Let go of Mary," Nolan said evenly.

"No," Titus said. He sounded like he was talking to someone about a bank transaction. He turned to Mary. "Do you want to go with him?"

"Uhm, yes. Yes, I do." She took her cue from Nolan, and she kept her tone even as well. It was like she knew not to poke the tiger.

"Mary, Mary, Mary...I already talked to you about the repercussions of what would happen if you didn't spend a little time with me and my friend." Titus turned to Nolan. "Now you have nothing to worry about. Who are you? Her boyfriend? It's fine. She's just going to spend a little bit of quality time with us, and then she'll come back to you. It's not like she was anything more than trailer trash to begin with, right?" Titus winked.

Rage, like he hadn't felt since he was a small child, surged through Nolan's body. That sneer, the tone, they were the same. How many times had Nolan heard this man, and that boy, call him and his mother trailer trash? He looked over at Maggie, who was so innocent and pure. Her face was chalk white but determined. She planned to keep herself together no matter what.

"Titus, I'm surprised you don't recognize me. It's Nolan O'Rourke."

Titus squinted and Arlo laughed. Of course Arlo laughed.

"You're not No-Good," Arlo scoffed.

"Arlo, where's Willie?" Nolan asked softly.

"He's serving twenty up at Riverbend."

"That's not going to be any fun," Nolan noted.

"Willie can handle it," Arlo stood up for his friend. "He's mean."

Nolan raised an eyebrow.

"You *are* Nolan," Titus said quietly. "I heard you joined the Army."

"Close enough. Now release Mary and we're going to leave."

Titus turned Maggie around so that she was looking at him. "I'll have that brat taken away from you by tomorrow night. Is that what you want?"

So that was his leverage.

"Let go of me, Titus," Maggie said as she pulled at her arm.

"If you don't get rid of your jarhead boyfriend, I'll arrange for the kid to be put in an orphanage and you to be thrown out of your trailer with all your shit, just like No-Good's slut of a mother was."

Nolan couldn't believe everything he'd heard, but enough was enough. He upended the small table separating him from the trio and Arlo confronted him holding a switchblade.

"Think you're a big man now, do you?" Arlo snickered.

"I've always hated your laugh," Nolan said. He grabbed Arlo's arm holding the knife and twisted his wrist and elbow in opposite directions, then he slammed his forearm down on his knee. He smiled with satisfaction when he saw the blood seeping through his long-sleeved shirt—proof that Nolan had given him a compound fracture. He kicked the knife across the office, then turned to Mary and Titus.

Mary was a couple of steps away from Titus, pulling what looked like money out from in between her breasts. She threw the bills on the ground.

"I don't want your filthy money," she bit out.

"Come here, Honey," Nolan held out his hand. She took the few steps necessary, then grabbed his hand like a lifeline. He pulled her to his side.

"Now, Titus, what am I going to do about you?" Nolan asked.

"You broke my arm," Arlo squealed.

Both Nolan and Titus growled 'Shut up' at the same time.

"I've always hated his laugh too," Titus grimaced.

"Shouldn't have made him your bestie, then," Maggie quipped.

Nolan laughed. "Good point, Mary."

"So you're back in town and found the trailer trash to date, figures." Titus's sneer was reminiscent of the past.

"Mary, what is it Titus and the whiner wanted?" Nolan asked as he turned to her. Despite her amusement, she was shaking.

"Titus said he was going to have Iris taken away from me if I didn't do what they wanted. We hadn't gotten to the part where they spelled things out, but I had a pretty good idea." Her lower lip was trembling.

He wanted to maim Titus just for that.

He turned to Titus.

"It's her word against mine, and nobody's going to believe her," Titus scoffed. He turned to Maggie, "Now you've—"

Nolan had him up against the wall before he could say another word. "Mary is mine, and you've made a big mistake. And do you know what else?" Nolan growled.

"What?" Titus jeered.

"Iris is mine too," he growled. "She's my sister, and nobody is taking her away from me."

"Like they're going to give a baby to some lowlife Army scum."

Nolan felt Maggie standing beside him. He gave

her a quick glance and she was smiling. "You're taking her?" Maggie was glowing.

"Damn right I'm taking her."

She turned to Titus. "He's a Navy SEAL. He's a medic. He makes things happen. If he says he'll take custody, he'll take custody." She looked over her shoulder at Nolan. "Right, Nolan?"

He grinned. "Right, Honey."

She took a step closer to Titus who had blanched at the mention of Nolan being a SEAL. She poked a finger into his chest. "And because he's a SEAL he can 'eff' you up." This time she didn't bother looking over her shoulder. "Right, Nolan?"

"It would be my ever-loving pleasure to 'eff' up this motherfucker."

Maggie giggled.

Titus held up his hands. "There's no need for violence," he said in a soothing voice.

"There's already been violence, he broke my arm," Arlo sobbed. "I'm bleeding. I need an ambulance!"

"Quit your whining," Titus shouted at him.

Nolan looked down at Arlo where he was lying on the floor. He put his boot on his broken arm and pressed while still continuing to hold Titus against the wall. Arlo shrieked.

"Please, please, please. Stop. I'm begging you."

"Give me dirt on Titus. Good dirt. Or I'll bust your kneecap."

Arlo looked at him in horror.

Nolan looked around the room and found what he

was looking for. "Honey, unplug that phone and bring over the cord to me, will you?" He smiled at how fast and easy Maggie caught on and did what he needed.

"Need me to tie up his hands?" She said as her chin tilted toward Titus.

"I've got this." He shoved Titus to the ground on his stomach and had him hog-tied ankles to wrists in one quick moment. Titus screamed for help.

"They're not going to hear you above that music," Nolan laughed. "What's more Kurt planned to give you plenty of alone time back here, didn't he?" Titus stopped yelling.

Nolan turned his attention to Arlo. He could threaten him with his gun, but he didn't want to. He really wanted to kick Titus, because that's what he used to do to him, but a little bit of information would take care of things.

"Arlo, tell me what you know," Nolan demanded as he started to prod at the man's left knee with his boot.

"I don't understand what you're asking."

"You don't know shit," Titus said. "If you want to live, you don't know shit," Titus yelled at his sidekick.

Well, now Titus deserved a kick.

Nolan kicked him, not hard enough to rupture anything, but hard enough so he wouldn't be able to catch his breath for a while, let alone talk. He saw Maggie jerk when he did it, and he looked up at her, worried she would be afraid of him now. Instead, she had a bit of a blood-thirsty smile on her face.

Go Maggie!

Nolan turned his attention to Arlo.

"What's Titus been doing? You don't tell me, and you'll be joining Willie with an arm and a knee that don't work so good, up in Riverbend."

"You've got nothing on me." Arlo whimpered.

"Mary, are you going to testify against Arlo for attempted rape?" Nolan asked.

"Darn right I am."

Nolan kicked at Arlo's knee harder, definitely leaving a bruise. "Talk."

"I'm telling you, I don't know anything."

This time Nolan picked him up by his broken arm and Arlo let out a high-pitched scream that could shatter glass.

"Please, don't hurt me anymore. I'll tell you. I'll tell you everything."

Nolan let him drop to the ground.

It took a few minutes for Arlo to quit sniveling and start talking. "Titus has been having me set fire to some cabins up near Stone Mountain, forcing those people to sell. He's planning on developing a resort out there with some feller—"

"Shut up!" Titus screamed hoarsely.

Nolan kicked Titus in the stomach, then kicked Arlo in the knee.

"How many cabins? How'd you do it?"

"Just three so far. I do it real slick. First I make sure nobody's home. I'm not going to murder anyone. You know?"

Nolan nodded. "How'd you set the fires?"

"I looked it up on the internet. I made them Moloto cocktails."

"Do you mean Molotov cocktails?" Nolan clarified.

"Yeah, them. They work slick as snot. I gotta do another cabin tomorrow night."

"You tell me which one and I'll get you your ambulance."

Nolan knew if he got this information to Gideon, he could backtrack everything back to Titus. There'd be something they could put him in jail for. He had no idea what, but Gideon would know.

He turned to Maggie. "You ready to mosey on outta here?"

"I'm thinking I get to burn my uniform now."

"We'll see," Nolan smiled. The miniskirt could definitely stay.

CHAPTER TWELVE

Since their original plans had them leaving Rowdy's at three a.m., they'd already made arrangements to stay at Trenda's house for the night, so that Bella could have her sleepover at the 'coolest hotel ever.' It was now midnight. Maggie waited on the doorstep, warm in Nolan's leather jacket as he 'swept' the area, before letting her in. Whatever that meant.

"Come on in, Honey," he said as he opened the front door back up, and pulled her in out of the cold night air.

"What does 'swept the area' mean?"

"It means I'm a paranoid bastard."

He'd set her little case near the couch, along with his partially filled duffle bag. "I found the guest room, as well as Trenda's room. Why aren't you sleeping in Trenda's room like she suggested?" Nolan asked.

"It seems intrusive. Sleeping on Bella's bed is fine

by me. I slept on a twin bed the entire time I lived in my father's house."

"Why don't you take the guest room? It has a double bed, and I'll take the couch," Nolan suggested.

Maggie laughed. "Nope."

"Hey, I thought you were supposed to be kind of submissive to men, what happened to that?"

"Didn't you hear? I turned over a new leaf." She smiled as she went to the kitchen to get a glass of water.

"That makes sense, you were pretty pushy with old Titus. Poking him in the chest and all."

Maggie smiled. "Yeah, that felt awesome. Almost as good as when you said you were going to protect and care for Iris. Did you mean it?"

Nolan walked up to where Maggie was standing next to the sink. They were almost touching. He looked down at her and his electric blue eyes glowed. "Damned right I meant it. She's my sister. I can't believe how much I've come to love her in just five days, there is no way she will ever end up in foster care."

Nolan rubbed the back of his neck. That was a sure sign he was either thinking about something or worried about something. "I've already done some research. If I can pass some evaluations from CPS, then I'll be allowed to adopt her. After that, how I handle things when I have to go out on a mission won't be their concern."

"But how *will* you handle it?"

"I'm not quite sure yet. I can't be the only single dad who's a SEAL. I'll find out how they're coping."

Even in the short time they'd been together, Maggie had come to realize how integral being a SEAL was to Nolan. He needed that job, but Iris needed a stable environment.

"Honey," Nolan prompted as he put his knuckles under her chin and lifted it so she was looking back up at him.

"What?" she asked quietly.

"Have you ever thought about moving close to me, so that maybe we could take care of her together?"

Maggie stepped back and Nolan dropped his hand. "That would never work."

"Why not?"

How could he even be asking this?

"Because I have to leave. I told you that."

"So, leave with me to Virginia."

"I can't." Her hair got into her face and she had to shove it off so she could see him in the dim light of the living room.

"Sure you can, Maggie. What's more, there are much better jobs you could get, and one of them would be a part-time nanny to Iris. I get paid well enough to pay for daycare, so this is perfect. Instead of paying daycare, I'd pay you."

She stepped forward and looked up into his face. "What part of *I have a psycho after me* did you not understand?" she yelled up at him.

"What part of *I'm a Navy SEAL* did you not understand?" He grinned down at her.

"You don't know what he's capable of." She could feel tears forming, and it made her mad. So mad.

"I do, Honey, I've listened to you. You told me how he cut you up that first time. I can't imagine it. I still want to get my hands on him for that. Now I assumed there was no way you could go to law enforcement. I understand he killed your dog and threatened your sister's little boy, but are you even sure he's still after you?"

I need to tell him, I need to tell him everything.

"He hurt Carla. Not too bad, because her neighbors got there in time. But he did."

"Who's Carla?"

"She's an online friend of my brother Brian's. She was the first person he sent me to after I left Elk Bay for the last time." Maggie set down her glass in the sink, then turned away from Nolan. She walked dejectedly over to Trenda's couch and sank down onto the soft cushions. It hurt just thinking about it.

"How is she? What did he do to her?"

"It scared her mostly. He gave her a black eye and split lip, but he tore her apartment apart." Maggie scrubbed the tears away. "She says she's okay. I can't call her on the burner phone, we agree that's too dangerous, but we connect on WeChat, and sometimes she sends me e-mails. She's dating someone now."

Nolan pulled the throw blanket from the back of

the couch, sat down, and then wrapped it around her. Maggie pulled it even tighter.

"I'm not making sense, am I?"

"Just tell me whatever you need to tell me." Even in the dim light, his eyes shone brightly. It was like the light from within them washed over her and protected her.

Boy, Maggie Celeste Rhodes, aren't you getting fanciful.

She giggled but it came out like a sob. She pushed away the blanket and reached out for Nolan.

"Aw, Honey, I've got you." With those words, she stopped reaching and just launched herself into his arms. He pulled her close, one big hand holding her head against his heart and she swore she heard it beating. He kissed the top of her head.

"I've got you. Nobody's going to hurt you ever again. I promise. I've got you."

I wish that were true.

She kept crying and he held her, stroking her hair with one hand, and the other rubbing comforting circles on her back. Lost in sorrow, she cried for herself, her dog, Jake, and the thought of leaving Iris, of leaving Nolan. She took comfort in Nolan's arms as she continued to sob.

───────

She needed to eat more. Nolan laid her down on the guest room bed and pulled off her shoes. He looked at her red hair spread out on the dark blue pillows and imagined how much prettier her blond hair would look.

She frowned, stretched, and wiggled. She looked uncomfortable as hell.

Aw, shit, it's the camisole.

"Maggie, wake up, Honey, you need to take off your camisole," he said softly.

"Go 'way." She slung an arm out at him, her fist connecting with his chest. He saw it more than felt it. He watched as she pulled at the camisole some more.

"Maggie, wake up," he said in a firm voice.

"Go 'way," she slurred.

"Well, shit."

He began unfastening the hooks, making a promise to himself that he would not look at anything other than the camisole. The more he tried to hurry his task along, the more he fumbled.

Shit.

Finally, he finished the last hook.

"So good," she sighed as she spread her arms wide.

Nolan pulled up the duvet cover and purposely did not notice her sweet pink nipples, or how her breasts were soft and ripe and he could easily cover them with just his palm. *No, I did not notice anything like that*, he thought as he made his way to the hall closet in hopes of finding some extra linens that he could use to sleep on the couch.

He found some and made up a pretty damn comfortable bed for himself. It was surprising that a woman with just a little girl would have such a big sofa, but maybe it was because she had such a big family. He'd heard a little bit about the Avery family growing up in Jasper Creek. The twins were two grades behind him. Zoe and Chloe were pretty girls. Nice, too. But he hadn't bothered to make friends with any of the Jasper Creek school kids since he knew he'd just be pulled out of the school and end up in foster care again, so what was the point?

He settled down for the night and knew he wasn't going to get a lick of sleep. He had to figure out how to convince Maggie that she didn't have to run anymore. Tomorrow morning, first thing, he'd sic Gideon on his Kyle's ass. Since this idiot had gone to college in International Falls, he had to have an electronic footprint. Chances were, with a little visit from Nolan and maybe a friend or two, he could be convinced to stay away from Maggie for good.

He needed to find out how long ago it was that he'd messed with her girlfriend, Carla. Hell, maybe Kyle had already given up.

He picked his phone up off the coffee table and sent Gideon a message to call him in the morning when he was in front of his computer. Now that Jada was living with him, he figured he slept in more often on the weekends.

"I can sure understand that," Nolan sighed.

A picture of Maggie on blue sheets, all pink, white, and perfect floated through his mind.

I saw nothing.

———

Did she smell coffee?

Who was Nolan talking to?

Maggie pushed back the covers and yelped.

"I'm naked!"

"Maggie, what's wrong?" Nolan yelled as he pushed open her bedroom door. Maggie had just enough time to pull the duvet cover up to her chin.

"I'm naked," she gulped.

He chuckled. "You're not naked. I just undid the camisole hooks so you could breathe. You were squirming around so much I could tell they were bothering you. I tried to wake you up so you could do it yourself, but you weren't having any of it."

Maggie frowned but she took better stock of herself and realized that her arms were still in the sleeves of the camisole, and her stockings and skirt were still on.

"I must have been dead to the world."

"Not quite. You tried to hit me when I was trying to wake you up."

"I did not," she protested primly.

"Did too." His grin got bigger.

Maggie was aghast. Except for Kyle, she'd never fought with anybody in her life. "I didn't hurt you, did I?"

"I think I might end up with a bruise."

"Oh no, where?" Maggie sat up straighter. She was just about to swing her legs out of the bed and get up when she realized she'd have to let go of the blanket.

She looked back up at Nolan and saw that he was silently laughing. "You're making fun of me," she accused.

"Only a little bit."

"So, I didn't hurt you?"

"No. I promise. It was the wimpiest hit of all time."

"Yeah, I'm not good at that. That's why I got a gun."

Nolan came into her room at that point. It was funny, even though she was half-naked under the covers, she didn't feel nervous having him in here.

Wait!

"You saw me naked."

"I didn't look," he said as he got closer to the bed.

She saw his little grin.

"You're grinning. You looked." *Oh, God.* Had he seen the mark that Kyle had cut into her? She looked at him and didn't see anything but that teasing little grin.

"I've been noticing *you* looking when I come back from a run all sweaty and my t-shirt is stuck to me."

Maggie thought her face would burst into flames because he was right. She needed to get this conversation on an even keel.

"Who were you talking to? Trenda? When are we doing the switch?"

"I said we'd bring over breakfast, from Polly's of course, you up for that?"

"Sure, as long as I get to wear a shirt of yours, or your leather jacket over my uniform when we get to the hotel. I don't want to be seen in my Rowdy's uniform first thing in the morning when I go through the lobby."

"I'll rustle something up for you."

Her little heart attack about being naked had been pretty damned cute. Nolan would bet his bottom dollar that he was the only man to have ever seen her breasts. The fact that she hadn't truly come unglued said a lot about how comfortable she was with him.

"What was that?" Nolan turned his attention to Trenda who was obviously speaking to him, and he'd missed it. He gave a quick glance over to Maggie and Bella who were on the floor working with Iris, teaching her to sit up.

"So, her name is Maggie, not Mary, huh?"

"What gives you that idea?" Nolan asked.

"Because you blew it twice during breakfast and called her that, and she didn't bat an eyelash."

Nolan went to rub his neck but stopped himself. Trenda was observant enough as was, he didn't need her analyzing his physical cues.

"Yeah, her name is Maggie. Still don't have her last name, though."

"You'll get it. She's smitten with you."

He tried to mask the shocked look on his face, but by the twinkle in Trenda's eyes, he'd obviously failed.

"Uhm, that's not how it is between us."

"Pity." Trenda picked up her cup of coffee and took a sip.

Yeah, it was a goddamned catastrophe as far as

Nolan was concerned, but until he got down to the bottom of things with her and got this idea of 'running' out of her head, he was not going to make a move. He refused to be one more person in the world who took advantage of Maggie Whomever.

Trenda tipped her head over toward where Maggie, Bella, and Iris were playing. "So how are you going to be handling things? What are your intentions?"

"First, I have to talk to my lieutenant about figuring out how to bring Iris from Tennessee to Virginia and adopt her. I don't think I'm going to be able to just buy a plane ticket, say she's my sister, and be on my way."

"No, I don't think that's going to work either. But why your lieutenant? Why not social services? I mean, my brother would definitely go to his, but why would you?"

"Who's Drake's lieutenant?" Nolan asked.

"Mason Gault. He has a way of figuring things out for his men."

"Kostya Barona is my lieutenant and figuring out the complicated is his specialty. I want to make sure that when I bring Iris to Virginia, we can work something out with my job that will allow me to spend the time I need with her to satisfy any Child Protective Service requirements."

"Sounds like a good plan. What else?" Trenda asked.

"I really want Maggie to come with me. To begin with, she can live with me before I help her find a place of her own."

"Have you mentioned it to her?"

"Yeah, she's not having any of it. She thinks that the guy she's running from will find her and we'll end up with a problem."

Trenda drew in a deep breath. "I always knew it was something like that. I gave her every opening possible to tell me what was going on. She can't live her entire life on the run, that's just nuts."

"I agree. What's more, she has a pretty powerful arsenal at her back now."

"Damn right. Not just you, but my brother would be happy to lend a hand."

Nolan liked how bloodthirsty Trenda sounded. It was very different from the Earth mother vibe she'd been giving off for most of the morning.

"If she's in Virginia, there's fourteen of us who'll have her back. That guy would wet his pants the first time he saw us." Nolan pointed to the last piece of bacon on his plate. "Would you like that?" he asked Trenda.

"No, I'm good, thanks though."

Nolan bit into the succulent bacon and chewed and thought about how to bring up what he needed to say.

"Just spit it out, O'Rourke, and I'm not talking about the bacon."

Nolan grinned.

"You know Titus Rutherford and Arlo Jackson?"

"Can we not talk about them, they're bad for my digestion," Trenda sighed. She took another sip of her coffee, then set it down on the table. "Aw, damn, by the look on your face, I see I don't have another choice. Okay, what's with those two assclowns?"

"I broke Arlo's arm last night. I highly doubt he'll go to the sheriff about it. Left Titus hogtied in the back office of Rowdy's—now he might go to the sheriff."

He liked the way Trenda's brown eyes sparkled. "I'm liking where this is going," she said. "Go on."

"I asked Arlo, in a very calm and loving manner, what kind of dirt he had on Titus."

"Oh, I'm sure you're as kind and loving as my brother in those kinds of situations. Only one broken arm, you say?" Trenda raised her eyebrow and Nolan chuckled.

"Titus might have a broken rib, not sure about that, but I digress. Arlo was extremely talkative last night. Turns out he's burned down three cabins out near Stone Mountain, and he was planning on doing another tonight."

Trenda shoved up from the table, startling Nolan and the three girls who were playing on the baby blanket.

"Are you okay, Mama?" Bella asked.

Trenda went over and kissed her daughter's forehead. "I'm just fine, Buttercup. Have you taught Iris to sit up yet?"

"No, but Mary says there's this toy." Bella frowned. "What is it again?" she asked Maggie.

"It's a baby walker, but she still needs to wait a few months before she's ready for that," Maggie told Bella with a smile. "We'll work on Iris sitting up and reading to her. It's good for her to hear us talking to her at this age. What do you think, do you want to do that?"

Trenda motioned for Nolan to join her on the balcony while Maggie kept her daughter and the baby occupied.

She turned around to talk to Nolan as soon as the sliding glass door was closed behind them. "Titus plans to develop around there, doesn't he?" she spat out the question.

"Yes," Nolan agreed.

"Bastard! We've had town halls where we've voted that down. Jasper Creek has set aside some of our taxes to buy some of the land out there, but we've been outbid by a corporation. The sheriff has been investigating the three houses burning down, and determined they were arson. I've got to let the sheriff know about this."

"Are you in good with the sheriff?"

"What do you mean by that, exactly?"

"Does he know you? Like you?"

"*She* knows me. *She* likes me. A few years back there was a big purge of our sheriff's department, including our sheriff. A woman named Alice Mitchell was brought in from Nashville to take over for a little bit, then she was voted in permanently in the following election. So yes, we get along. What do you need me to do? Is this about you breaking Arlo's arm and Titus's broken rib?"

"Yep. If we put pressure on Titus about the development, they might push back on assault."

"If they wait too long, and haven't pressed charges, I would think their cases lose weight, wouldn't they?" Trenda asked.

"I'm not sure," Nolan sighed. "That's why I wanted to know about your relationship with the sheriff."

"Tomorrow, when I drop Bella off at school, I'll go visit Alice. Besides what Arlo said, do you have any more information?" Trenda asked.

"I will by tomorrow morning. I won't be here though. I have to fly back early tomorrow, and check in with my team Monday afternoon."

"We'll be here waiting for you."

Trenda reached up and kissed him on the cheek. "You're a good big brother."

CHAPTER THIRTEEN

Maggie wasn't sure what to do with herself now that Iris was fed and down for her nap. She wanted to ask Nolan what he was talking to Trenda about on the balcony.

She absolutely *did not*, in *no way, not on God's green earth*, want to talk about him being sweaty after a run or her almost naked in bed.

She fiddled with the nicest pair of jeans she had and the lavender sweater that actually fit her smaller form. She kind of felt uncomfortable wearing a top that molded her breasts, but at the same time, she wanted to look halfway decent, and not in a slutty, Rowdy's sort of way. Her feet were cold so she put on a pair of fuzzy socks, bright purple. She stepped out into the common living area.

Nolan wasn't there.

Maggie laughed. She'd psyched herself up for nothing.

Figures.

She went back into her bedroom and snagged her phone and her wireless earbuds. She had another biography she wanted to listen to, all about General Patton. What she'd heard so far she really liked. Despite being a general, he was in no way bloodthirsty. No, he was always thinking strategically. He would think about how today's decisions would impact tomorrow's outcomes. He was brilliant. She wanted to learn from him. She needed to be thinking strategically. There was now only one more state between Arizona and Tennessee, and that was when she lived in Oklahoma. There, she'd thought she'd had the perfect job as a nanny, until the Coopers' marriage imploded that one weekend.

She didn't think she needed to warn them since Jenny Cooper moved with her kids to Boston and Mr. Cooper moved to San Francisco. Talk about leaving a cold trail. It was also the reason she had moved without much of a plan, but she had had money, so that was a good thing. She was able to afford to buy a car from their gardener, so no more Greyhound buses for her.

This time she had a little bit of time to think and plan and she was going to make use of it. Tomorrow was Monday, and she would be chatting with Brian so she could tell him everything that was going on. Maybe he would have some ideas on what they could do about their paperwork. It would make life a lot easier if she could get a driver's license and a social security card. Maybe he'd have an idea of how she could check on

Jake's status without alerting Kyle. Also, she would tell him that her e-mail account was not secure, and maybe he would set up a new one for her.

Her head was spinning with plans and ideas by the time she settled down in the corner of the couch and started listening to her book.

"What?!" Maggie's phone went flying when she felt something pull on her foot. She opened her eyes and saw Nolan looking at her with regret, right before he picked her phone up off the floor. Thank God it was carpeted.

Maggie pulled out her earbuds. "You scared me to death."

"I got that," Nolan said ruefully. He handed Maggie her phone. "I didn't mean to. I'd said your name a couple of times, but that wasn't getting through."

Maggie swung her legs around so she was sitting upright. "I do tend to get caught up in the books I'm listening to."

"Seem to. Listening to Thomas Jefferson again?"

"General Patton. I want to learn the art of war." She grinned.

"Not a bad guy to learn it from." Nolan nodded as he sat down beside her.

Shoot, he was wearing another tight white t-shirt. She hated and loved those things.

Get your mind out of the sewer!

Telling herself that didn't help. Not when the shirt lovingly formed to the muscles of his chest and abdomen. She'd seen some men with their shirts off during summer as they worked in the fields, but none of the men in Elk Bay had a body like Nolan O'Rourke's.

"That's a pretty sweater you're wearing."

She loved the sound of his voice, with his honeyed Southern accent. She especially liked it when he was saying something nice about how she looked.

Oh God, I have a crush on him!

Maggie winced. She didn't have time for a girlish crush, she needed to get some money together and figure out the next place she was going to go!

"You're thinking awfully hard," Nolan teased.

"I'm trying to remember what my sweater looks like, is all."

"It's purple, and it's not baggy like all the other things you own." Now Nolan's eyes were actually sparkling.

I'm doomed.

"Oh, yeah. *That* sweater. Uhm, what were you and Trenda talking about out on the balcony?"

"The business that Titus has going on. She's going to talk to the sheriff in town."

"Are you going to get into any trouble?"

"Nah, she doesn't think so. Anyway, it doesn't sound like Titus has made any friends around here, so nobody's going to be working real hard to take his side."

"But what about Arlo? He must have gone to the hospital to get his arm taken care of."

"The number of people who like Titus?" Maggie

nodded. "Divide that number by five, and that would be how many people like Arlo. Yeah, I'm in the clear."

Maggie let out a deep breath; she hadn't even been aware of how worried she'd been. "Does she think they'll be arrested?"

"We didn't get into that. But it seemed hopeful. I didn't see a lot of justice being handed out here in Jasper Creek when I was growing up. I don't know how it works now."

For once, Nolan didn't seem bitter talking about his past. Maybe now was a good time to approach him about his mom—after all, they *did* have a deal. But maybe it would be easier if she took the roundabout approach.

"What was it like here in Jasper Creek when you were growing up?"

She saw him pause. "Did you know Trenda or any of her siblings? I know she has a big family."

"Yeah, I knew her twin sisters. They were a couple of years behind me in school, but we didn't talk much. I never knew when I was going to be home or not, so I didn't make friends here. Or anywhere, really."

Maggie frowned. "That doesn't seem like you. I mean sure, you came off as pretty antisocial to begin with, but I've heard you on the phone with all of your teammates, and you all sound like you're having the best times ever. I love all the laughter. I don't know about their sides of the conversations, but you seem to laugh and swear a lot. I'm assuming they do too?"

"Yep, we use the 'eff' word and everything," Nolan said with a big 'ole grin. "Wanna try it?"

"I'll pass," she said primly. "How many men on your team?"

"There's fourteen of us at the moment."

"Why do you say it like that?"

"I think Sebastian is going to ask for a job where he's not in the field anymore. We haven't discussed it, but I've been over to his house a few times when his baby son, Neil, has had the croup, and his wife is currently on bedrest with their second child, and I can see it's eating him up. Right now he's on leave, but my guess is he's going to want to stay close to Gianna and his kids, not running around across the world. I think he'll ask for a desk job."

Maggie bit her lip and thought about Iris, but that wasn't what she wanted to talk about right now. She wanted to talk about his childhood.

"So, you were a loner as a child, but you were able to build strong friendships as an adult. That must have been tough to learn."

"Am I on your psychiatrist couch?" he mocked.

"I'm just impressed with how well you were able to come out of such a hard childhood. Ginger told me about how she was after you turned four, and how miserable it was for you."

"What do you mean after I turned four? You make it sound like she was a good mother before then, and I know that wasn't true."

"Do you? Do you really? You don't remember a time when she was good to you?"

Nolan shot off the couch and paced over to the balcony window. He didn't look at her as he started talking. "What I remember is having to hide under my bed when she had men over cause she was turning tricks. That's what I remember. And why was she doing that? Cause she was shooting up. The first memory I have of Ginger is me crawling out from underneath my bed, I couldn't have been more than four years old. I'd been cowering there with my stuffed green hippopotamus named Rover. I came out of my room because I'd finally heard the front door slam shut and a loud motor sound of someone leaving. Looking back, it was probably somebody on a bike."

Nolan turned around and Maggie saw the wild look of suffering in his eyes. She knew the story was going to get much worse.

"I come out, Ginger's not even in her bedroom, she's on the living room couch. She's got a blanket partways covering her naked body, but she's passed out, and I'm worried she'll be cold. I cover her up and put Rover next to her because he always makes me feel better. I get some juice out of the fridge because there's not any milk. I bring it back to her and try to get her to drink some, but she doesn't wake up."

Maggie got up off the couch and walked over to him, then wrapped her arms around his waist and leaned her head back so she could look into his eyes.

"I remember not wanting to go back to my room

without Rover, and I want my Mama to have Rover if she's dead. So I sit next to the couch all night. I don't remember what happened the next morning. Something must have, because she didn't die. What I do know? I never remember seeing Rover again."

Maggie had no idea what to say to that.

They stood in silence for a long time, her head resting against his heart.

"Aw, Honey, don't cry. It was years and years ago. It's in the past."

But that was the problem, wasn't it? There was a part of Nolan that still had 'no trespassing' signs posted all around him. She'd asked him two days ago if he'd ever been married. When he'd told her no and he'd told her he'd never even had a long-term girlfriend, this was why. Was he destined to live his life as cold, lonely, and scared as that little boy?

"But that isn't who Ginger was, not always," she whispered into the soft cloth of his t-shirt.

He tilted her chin up, then used his thumbs to wipe away her tears. "I get that, Maggie," he whispered. "I believe you, Honey."

"You might believe me, but it's not enough, is it?" Her heart hurt so badly for him. "She broke you, didn't she?"

His eyebrows rose. "What are you talking about?" He was seriously curious. "I'm not broken. I'm damned happy with my life. And in this past week, I'm happier than ever, because I now have Iris in my life. In just five days she's stolen my heart and I can't imagine my life without her in it."

Maggie dropped her head onto his chest. He had the most beautiful soul imaginable, she just wanted more for him. She so wished he would open up his heart to believe in love. Scratch that, to *trust* in love.

"She loved you," Maggie whispered. "Your mama loved you."

Nolan stiffened beneath her.

"She might have told you a lot of things, Maggie. She might even have believed them in the end, but I know the woman I grew up with. She didn't love me. I was a pebble in her shoe that did nothing but cause her foot to bloody. I was more than a nuisance; my very existence caused her pain."

"Is there anything I can say to convince you otherwise?"

He thought back to that flashback he'd had in Polly's parking lot. Was that true, or just the work of an overactive, hopeful, imagination?

"Why are you working so hard to convince me? Why does it matter so much to you? I would understand if she were alive, and you were trying to mend fences between the two of us, but she's not. Why not leave it like it is?"

Maggie lifted her head back so she was looking up at him again. She really was just a pixie of a woman. A beautiful fairy. He could get lost in her seaglass-green eyes. "I think this holds you back from being truly happy, and I want you to be truly happy, Nolan."

He gave her his most charming grin. "I am, Honey. I have the world by the tail. Hell, I even have a beautiful woman in my arms." He waggled his eyebrows. "Hey, hey, Honey. No more tears. Why are you crying again?"

"You're lying to me. Have you ever been in love?"

"Of course not," he said indignantly. "I bet you haven't either, have you?"

"No, but at least I'm open to the idea."

He gripped her tighter. The idea of her in love with some mysterious man did not make him happy. "How could you want to be in love with someone after watching those assholes from your hometown, especially Kyle? I thought you would be running away from love like it was the plague."

Maggie sighed and shifted in his arms. She brought one hand up and held it over his chest. "My sister Catherine, even though she was forced into a marriage that she didn't want, she ended up in love with Rainier. Yeah, he's twenty years older, but he's a good man, and they've made a good life for themselves. I've seen it. I've met Trenda's sister Evie and her husband Aiden, those two radiate love. One day, I want something like that in my life. If..."

"If what?"

She turned her head to the side. "Never mind."

"No, tell me."

She pulled out of his arms. "I need to check on Iris."

"You just put Iris down a half hour ago. She'll be down for at least another hour and a half. Now tell me what you were going to say."

"I was just being fanciful," she said as she moved toward the counter with the microwave. She straightened up the coffee fixings. Nolan came up behind her and blocked her in.

"Answer the question, Maggie. You want love in your life *if*. If what?"

She spun around to look at him. "If I survive. All right? If I survive!"

Nolan stood there in shock. This was the first moment he realized that she took this as a life-and-death situation. Fuck, he hadn't made it clear that he was going to protect her?

I'm a fucking dumbass.

He put his arm around her and guided her back to the couch. She was shivering, so he cuddled her up onto his lap and was so thankful when she didn't resist.

"Maggie, I need you to listen to me, okay? Kyle is never going to get to you again, I promise you. You know what I do for a living. There isn't a chance in hell he is going to get through me to you. I won't allow it."

She didn't say anything, just burrowed closer, her head underneath his chin, her arms clamped around his chest. He couldn't stand the way she was shivering. Couldn't stand it.

"Talk to me, Maggie."

"You don't understand, Nolan. You don't get it."

He stroked her hair. She'd left it down, so he combed his fingers through the silky strands, making sure to caress her scalp and stroke her tense neck.

"What don't I get?"

"You won't know when he's coming, and he won't just come at you. He'll do something like he did to Jake."

"Jake?"

Who the hell is Jake?

"Jake Sanders, my boss at the dude ranch in Arizona. Kyle sabotaged his car. Jake is lucky to be alive."

"When did this happen?"

"The article was dated two weeks ago. That's how he'll come at you, Nolan. Or worse, he'll do something to Iris."

She started to struggle. He thought it was to get out of his arms, but then he realized it was so she could look up at him. She grabbed at his head, clasping both of his cheeks. "He'll kill you if I stay."

"I'm not going to stay, Maggie. You, me, and Iris are going to go to Virginia. I'm going there tomorrow and get things sorted so the two of you can follow. I'm going to work it all out."

"I need to leave now."

"When did you leave Arizona?"

"Almost two years ago."

Nolan relaxed. "So you stayed somewhere between the dude ranch and Jasper Creek?"

She nodded.

"There you go then. We've got plenty of time to track him down. Don't worry, we'll get his ass. You're going to be fine. I promise you."

"You're not thinking right, he has my e-mail address. Think about it, Nolan. Now he has a way to trace me."

"I'll have my buddy Gideon look into it. You're right, that is something, but if your brother set it up right, it shouldn't matter. What matters is him following a path. He still has to find your next stop. So we have time. I'll stop him with my team."

She stopped struggling. "You think so?"

"I don't think so, I know so. We take care of the bad guys, this is what we do."

She slumped against him.

"Oh, Nolan, I so want to believe you."

"Then believe. Believe."

CHAPTER FOURTEEN

Nolan talked Maggie into taking a nap while Iris was sleeping. He told her he had to make some phone calls. After everything that they had talked about, she was more than happy to do so. She was exhausted.

She kind of remembered Nolan coming into her bedroom to get Iris when she cried, but he told Maggie to keep sleeping, so she did. Now it was dusk and she saw Iris was back in her crib dressed in her little pink jammies. When she went and investigated, she saw that Iris's hair was slightly damp.

"Good job, Nolan," she said in a whisper. He'd given Iris a bath.

Maggie went over to the dresser. She picked up her sweater and jeans off the top and took them into the bathroom where she took care of business, then got dressed again to see what Nolan was up to. She found him asleep on the couch with one of the tiny bottles of hotel scotch and a half-filled glass on the coffee table beside him. Even more interesting was an envelope addressed to Nolan from Ginger, one marked RETURN TO SENDER. But Maggie saw that it had been opened, and by the looks of it, he'd read both pages.

She assumed it was the last letter Ginger had sent to Nolan before she passed away, since Maggie had the rest of them in her trailer, and she'd read them all. All the letters put together pretty much explained Ginger's side of the story of how Nolan grew up. It put Ginger in a pretty bad light, but the ones she wrote the last year and a half had a different tone. Instead of rehashing the past and asking for forgiveness, it told Nolan about her current life. About how she'd turned her life around, and about the man who had been her sponsor at Narcotics Anonymous.

Burt Ketchum had been a troubled man before he finally got sober. He had a family that he had left, and two sons who still wouldn't talk to him. Ten years after abandoning his family, he found a life in Jasper Creek and got a job as a mechanic at Floyd's garage. Eventually, he became Ginger's sponsor and he was her rock. Their relationship didn't turn romantic until she'd been sober for four years. When Maggie had met him, he and Ginger had been together for years, but now he was living with Ginger and she was taking care of him as he was fading away from brain cancer. When they realized that Ginger was pregnant, they thought it was a miracle. Before he died, he and Ginger had agreed not to give Iris his last name. Burt didn't want his adult sons to be involved in Iris's life. Ginger had reluctantly agreed.

Ginger had been six months pregnant and suffering from diabetes and high blood pressure when they laid Bart to rest. The only time Maggie cried harder was the morning Ginger died.

"I read it," Nolan said in a hoarse voice.

Maggie turned from the letter and looked at Nolan. He looked ravaged.

"What'd it say?"

"She talked a lot about you. She said that you were an angel, that after losing Burt she would have given up if it hadn't been for you."

Maggie watched as Nolan swung his legs over the side of the couch and pushed himself into a sitting position. She could see the dried tear tracks on his face.

"She was a light in my life too. It went both ways. I just wish..."

"What? What do you wish, Honey?"

"That she had a chance to see what a good man you've turned into."

Nolan's elbows hit his knees and he dropped his head into his hands. "I fucked up." He whispered. "How am I going to be able to live with myself?"

Maggie dropped to her knees in front of him and pulled his hands away from his face. "Your mother did nothing but say great things about you. She was so proud of you, Nolan. She told me all the time about how you rose above all the sh...stuff you grew up with and went on to be a good man in the Navy."

"But I never listened to her, I never bothered to read one of her goddamned letters." His blue eyes were awash with tears. "It's too late to make it up to her."

Maggie watched as one tear trickled down his cheek and settled at the side of his mouth. She wiped it away. He turned his head and kissed her thumb.

"She just wanted *you* to forgive *her*. Do you?"

"I don't even know who my father is. Somebody got a fifteen-year-old girl pregnant, and her parents kicked her out, but she kept me. How could I not forgive a young woman like that? Of course I do."

Maggie squeezed his hands tight. "Oh, Nolan, you impress me more each hour."

Nolan grabbed hold of the hand that he'd kissed. "I lied. I had an earlier memory of my mom, not just the one with my toy hippo. She was getting me to eat my vegetables so I could have a brownie she baked for me. Her hair was washed and she smelled good."

"When did you remember that?"

"The first night I picked up food at Polly's. I think the drugs came later. I really wish that she had been that mom all the time."

"She loved you so much, Nolan. So, so much. The drug use was an illness, and you got caught up in the spiral."

Nolan closed his eyes and nodded as he kissed the palm of her hand. "I just wish I could have made peace with her when she was alive."

"My sweet man, you are doing something even better, you are taking care of her little baby. She's smiling from heaven, she couldn't ask for a better son."

"I hope so."

"I know so. Because I've never met a better man on this earth than you."

He was. He was the best man she knew, and she wanted him to know it. She wanted him to feel it. Who was she kidding? She just wanted *him*.

Tentatively, Maggie moved her other hand and cupped the back of Nolan's head. She watched his face to make sure he wasn't going to reject her, but she didn't see rejection, she saw curiosity.

She lifted up higher on her knees so that she could get even closer to him. She'd fantasized about his mouth and now was her chance to taste it. He'd be leaving in the morning. This was her one and only chance.

Her lips hovered over his as she stared into his eyes, and then one side of his mouth tipped up and his eyes heated. With one free hand, she pulled his head closer and pressed her lips against his. He tasted salty, and she realized it was from tears. Then she realized that his firm mouth was actually soft and welcoming. She'd had no idea just how long she'd wanted—no needed—to taste him, and it was better than all of her hopes.

His lips parted, and then he took over. He drove his fingers into her hair and brought her even closer to him, and then growled—actually growled—into her mouth as he licked at her bottom lip until she opened wider. His tongue thrust into the warm cavern of her mouth and she sucked him in even deeper. He tugged at her hair and the tiny pain felt so good, she did the same thing to him, and he growled again. She tugged her other hand out of his, and dug her fingers into his t-shirt, right over his heart.

She ripped her mouth away from his. "Take off your shirt," she demanded.

Nolan felt like he was in freefall—he'd never experienced this with a woman, not ever. He stared at Maggie. Once again, she wasn't wearing any make-up, and she was the most beautiful woman he'd ever seen. Her eyes glowed like seaglass, and it was as if she could see into his soul.

He stroked his fingers down her cheek. "We need to take this slow."

"I don't want to. You're leaving tomorrow."

He closed his eyes, trying to get himself under control, and jumped when she bit his bottom lip. She held onto his lip for a moment and lashed it with her tongue. That sensation went straight to his cock.

"God, you pack a punch."

"So do you, Nolan. Please take off your T-shirt."

"I'm not sure that's a good idea," he demurred.

She leaned backward on her knees and pulled off her lavender sweater and flung it over the arm of the couch. Her red hair went wild. He'd never seen a more beautiful woman.

God, I need her.

"Oh God," she mumbled, then she slammed her arms around herself and turned around.

"Are you okay?" he asked in a frantic voice. What in the hell was wrong?

Maggie shuffled with her back to him, edging toward where her sweater was. Then she picked it up and draped it in front of her, covering her ribs, not her bra.

"This was a bad idea," she whispered. "Well, maybe not a bad idea. But the naked part is bad." She turned her back to him again and put her sweater back on.

"Maggie, is this about the scar I saw?"

"You saw it?" she gasped.

He got up and put his arms around her. "I did, Honey. You told me about it, remember? I'm not sure if making love so soon is the right thing to do, but if we do...and we do it naked...you're going to see scars on my body too."

She turned tear-filled eyes up at him. "It's so ugly, Nolan."

"It's not ugly. It's just a scar. You're beautiful, and everything about you is beautiful."

"Really?"

"But, Maggie, we've only known each other six days, Honey. I think this proves it's too soon."

He watched as she swallowed and took off her sweater again, then thrust back her shoulders. His fingers reached out and reverently traced the 'V' on her ribcage under her right breast.

"His last name is VanWyck, that's what the 'V' stands for."

"No, it doesn't, Maggie. It stands for valiant and victorious."

"Really?" she breathed.

"Absolutely."

He got down on his knees and showered her scar with kisses.

She shoved at his shoulders, and he let himself fall back on the sofa. "After saying what you just said, don't tell me this is wrong. I am sick and tired of men telling me what I should and shouldn't do. I'm twenty-one years old. I might have been sheltered when I first left Elk Bay, but two and a half years on the run changes things."

He watched as she started to unbutton her jeans.

"Wait a minute."

"No!"

"Maggie, if you just want to lose your virginity—"

"Nolan O'Rourke, you listen to me, and you listen good. If I had just wanted to get...get...uhm...laid, I could have a lot sooner than this." He looked at her bright red face and regretted what he'd just said.

"That's not what I'm saying."

"What *I'm* saying is that you are a sweet and special man, and I want to make love with you." Suddenly her hands dropped away from the front of her jeans. "Unless you don't want me," she said quietly.

Nolan stood up so fast, Maggie was forced to take a step backward and she almost fell over the coffee table.

He caught her. "Not want you? I want you so bad I'm burning up. But you deserve someone who is going to marry you."

She clutched at his forearms. "Eventually, yes I do. But right now, I hope I've been good enough to deserve you," she whispered.

"Holy fuck." She damn near took him to his knees with that statement. Was she kidding? How could she even think something like that?

"Maggie, you shine. Your soul is like a pure diamond that just spreads light and joy, I'm never going to be worthy of you."

"Nolan—"

"But that's not going to stop me. I've been given very few gifts in this life, but when I get one I know enough to take it, treasure it, and thank the good Lord above for it. You're my gift."

Her hands went back to the top button of her jeans, her eyes twinkling. "So that means yes?"

"Oh yes, it means yes."

He swept her up in his arms and stepped over the coffee table to get to his room quicker. He didn't know how long they'd have until Iris woke up, but he wanted as much time as possible to pleasure his beloved Maggie.

For a moment he thought about just how old the condom in his wallet was, and realized it wasn't quite over two years, so it should be fine.

The bed had been made up, and there was chocolate on the pillows, which he avoided as he laid

Maggie onto the center of the king-sized bed, then he laid on his side next to her. Even with the white sheets, he couldn't help but imagine what she would look like with blond hair spilling all around her head.

She'd be gorgeous.

"What? Why are you looking at me like that?"

"Because you're gorgeous, and I can't believe you're in my bed."

"So are you." She bit her bottom lip and frowned.

"What, Honey?"

"Are you going to take off your shirt now?" she asked shyly.

Nolan realized that the temptress who was out in the living room had disappeared. That was all right, he'd take care of all versions of his Maggie.

"Honey, I'll do whatever you want, this is your show. Do you understand that?"

She frowned again and shook her head.

"How new is this to you, Maggie?" He waited for a response. When none was forthcoming, he asked again. "You've been kissed before me, right?"

Please say yes, please say yes.

She nodded her head.

"What else, Honey?"

"That's it. That's why it's silly for it to be my show. Shouldn't you be showing me?"

Well, she's got me there.

"How about we go back to kissing, and you tell me if there's something you don't like, and also tell me if there's something you do like?"

"Nolan O'Rourke, I've already told you what I want, and you're not darned listening to me. Take off your darned shirt!"

Nolan burst out laughing as she shoved him onto his back.

So much for shy.

"I really need to teach you how to swear, Maggie."

"That is not what you need to be teaching me right now," she said as she pulled at the hem of his t-shirt.

He set her gently aside and sat up, then pulled his t-shirt up over his head. "Is that better?"

Her eyes were wide open, and he never felt more wanted.

"I get to touch you, right?"

"Absolutely. Actually, I insist." He caught her wrists and brought her hands to his chest so that she could see how hot his skin was. As soon as her palms rested flat against his torso, he shuddered.

"That happened to me when you touched me out in the living room. You liked that, didn't you?"

"Oh yeah, Maggie. I love it when you touch me."

"We're going to have a lot of fun, aren't we?"

"Oh yeah. But now it's my turn."

CHAPTER FIFTEEN

He started with a kiss. He licked her lower lip before sinking his tongue into her mouth and stroking it against hers. She jolted, it was as if electricity arced between them, and it had her panting.

He tasted so good and she needed more. She needed the kiss to go even deeper. When he thrust his tongue into her mouth again, she captured it and suckled it, and arched into him when she heard his groan of delight. Then he was kissing, demanding, thrusting, and giving her exactly what she craved.

Maggie tried to clench him closer as need roared through her, but then she felt his hand stroking from her waist, up to her breast. She trembled with excitement, wishing and hoping that he would touch her there, then he did. He closed his big hand over her breast and gently squeezed and this time she moaned—and it was with delight as well.

"The bra needs to go, Maggie."

"Yes," she whispered in agreement.

Would he kiss her breasts? She heard that on some of the books she'd listened to and it sounded sexy. The women liked it.

"Nolan, I want you to kiss me on my breasts after you take off my bra, is that okay?"

"You are fucking unreal, my Maggie. I've never been this close to losing it before."

Maggie clenched his biceps, her fingernails digging deep.

That didn't sound good.

"What's wrong?" he suddenly asked.

"Was it wrong I asked?"

"Fuck no. It's fucking great you asked. You ask for anything and everything you can think of. I want to take you to the moon tonight."

Maggie felt him drag her bra straps off her arms, and now she was naked from the waist up. "You're gorgeous. Absolutely beautiful."

Maggie felt herself blush underneath his intent regard. Then his hands came up and cupped both of her full breasts, and his thumbs brushed over her nipples.

"Nolan," she cried out. The sensation overwhelmed her.

"Before a kiss, I think a lick."

She watched as he bent his head and swirled his tongue around her right nipple. It was as if all of her nerve endings had coalesced to that one spot on her body. She stayed as still as she could, not wanting to even breathe, just wanting to savor this one perfect moment. Then he did something she wasn't anticipating.

When his lips opened up and surrounded her nipple and tasted, then suckled, she caught fire, crying out his name again and again. Slowly he let her go and kissed his way back up her body so he could look into her eyes.

"How are you doing?" he asked, his blue eyes smoldering.

"I'm doing fantastic," she sighed. "Let's do more things."

"Yeah?"

"Oh yeah," she said as she wound her arms around his neck. "And then do you know what?"

He shook his head, "No, what?"

"After that, we should do more things, and more things, and even more things, 'cause I think you're probably really good at this."

Nolan shouted with laughter.

"God, Maggie, I hope I am, because you're blowing me away."

She frowned. "But I haven't done anything."

"The way you touch me, the way you respond? Honey, you're amazing."

A slow smile spread across her face. "That's good then. Because I want us to take off all of our clothes next."

"I can get down with that."

She loved the way he smiled, especially when he had a little bit of stubble. It made him look all pirateish. Was that a word? Who cared, it was now. He slid his hands down her torso, and finally, the button on her jeans was released and he was unzipping her jeans.

"Wait a minute!" she almost shouted.

"What's wrong?" his head shot up to look her in the eye.

"Uhm, you can't look."

"Honey, we've already been through this once. I told you we're going to have a problem making love if I can't look."

"I don't mean about me being naked, just don't look at my panties, okay?"

"Nope." He finished unzipping her jeans and pulled them off her body, then he sat on his haunches and grinned down at her panties. At least he didn't laugh.

"Daffy Duck, huh?"

"He's my favorite."

Nolan palmed her breasts and she undulated upwards. Then his hands trailed downwards until they were at the elastic of her panties. "You've sold me; Daffy is now my favorite cartoon character too," he said as he slipped her undies down off her legs.

Maggie shivered. Even though it was her idea to get naked, it was still a lot to get used to. She looked up at his face for reassurance and there he was, looking right back at her face—such a look of warmth and support.

Once again, Maggie realized that she'd never felt so safe or cared for, even now at her most vulnerable.

"You good?" he asked.

"I'd be better if I weren't the only naked person in this bedroom," she whispered wantonly.

Nolan got up off the bed and stood up, then quickly took off his jeans and briefs. Except for little boys that she babysat for, Maggie had never seen a naked man, and little boys definitely... *Did. Not. Count.*

She took a few moments to think about the mechanics of intercourse, but then remembered women had babies. So this had to work. Somehow. Right?

"Maggie, mine. You look scared to death," Nolan said as he sat back down on the bed.

"Well, if you were going to be on the receiving end of your penis, you'd be scared too." She shot out a hand and covered his mouth before he had a chance to laugh. "No laughing."

He kissed her fingers. "No laughing, I promise." Nolan cleared his throat. "So no mother-daughter talk? No sister-to-sister talk?"

"Gosh no. We wouldn't talk about sexual intimacy."

"Well, we will. You asked me to kiss your breasts. Why? Why did you know about that?"

"It was in a book I listened to."

"Was there anything else in that book that sounded good to you?"

Maggie tried to keep her eyes on Nolan's face as they were talking, but she couldn't help sneaking peeks at his penis. It was too big. It wasn't supposed to be like that, was it?

"I know they made love, but they just said they came together and it was wonderful. I wanted to do that. Wait, I mean I still want to, but I'm just kind of worried."

Nolan cupped her cheek. "I can't give you the mother-daughter talk. But I can give you the talk that I gave to a new recruit once. Do you want to hear that?"

"Was he a virgin?"

Nolan nodded his head.

"Okay, what did you tell him?"

"First, I told him that having sex with a partner is more than just him finding an orgasm. This should be a time when you have more consideration about the other person than yourself. I told him that despite what anyone tells you, sex should only happen when your emotions are involved, when there is respect and care on both sides. I told him not to take advantage of someone, and don't let yourself be taken advantage of."

"That doesn't say much about what to do, though," Maggie complained.

Nolan smiled. "I'm not done yet."

Then he continued. "I told Eddie, with those things in mind, it will come easy to you to remember to always, always bring and use protection. Then I explained he should always make sure to listen and watch what makes your partner happy, and ensure that they are satisfied before you are. If at any time they want to stop, you respect that. In the end, I said that if he remembered these things, ninety-nine percent of the time he'd end up with a very enjoyable experience."

"But that still doesn't explain specifics. I mean at least in my book I knew that it would be nice if you kissed my breasts... but then you made it even better when you..."

"When I took your nipple into my mouth and sucked on it."

Maggie thought her hair would catch on fire she was so embarrassed.

"Yeah, that. So didn't you tell him other things, more specific things?"

"Honey, guys his age had been looking at Playboys for years."

"What are Playboys?"

"Ah, Maggie, how about if I show you some things, instead of more talking?"

She gulped. "Will I like them?"

"If at any point you don't like something, all you have to do is tell me to stop. Does that sound good?"

She nodded. "But Nolan, try to only do good things, okay?"

"Yes, ma'am."

She giggled. Yep, this had some really good potential.

How could she be a shy virgin, a smartass, and such a passionate siren?

I have no idea, but I fucking love it!

He thought about getting under the duvet to cover his erection, but then she'd be covered up and he sure as hell didn't want that. Well, there was one thing he could do to hide his cock, and it would give them both a whole hell of a lot of pleasure.

"Lie back, honey."

A confused frown crossed her face. "Why? I want to kiss you again," she said as she reached for him.

Nolan easily pressed her gently back onto the pillows. "I want to kiss you too, Honey. I just want you lying down while I do that, okay?"

"Yes," she moaned as his mouth covered hers.

What started out slow and sultry, soon turned into wet and wild. When she bit his bottom lip again, he laughed into her mouth. "You're a bloodthirsty little thing, aren't you?"

"I can't help it," she whined. "I just get caught up in everything and feel so much. It's the same reason I keep scratching you, it doesn't make any sense."

"Yes, it does, Baby. Your body is just getting overwhelmed, it needs some sort of release. Let's see what I can do about that."

She pushed back the hair from his forehead. "I don't want to hurt you," she said.

"You know it's going to hurt a little bit when we make love for the first time, don't you?"

She nodded.

Thank God, somebody had at least explained that to her.

"But after that, it will only feel good, I promise."

This time it was her own lip that she bit. "Okay, Nolan."

He gave her another long kiss, then made his way down her body until he was kissing her slightly rounded stomach. Her skin was like warm silk. He slid his hands around to her back and did something he'd been longing to do since he'd seen her in that red mini-skirt—he squeezed her heart-shaped ass.

Maggie arched up, and Nolan took that opportunity to push her legs apart with his torso and slide his body between them. He continued kissing her tummy, delighting in her shivers. Poor girl had no idea what was coming next. Slipping his big hands even lower, he gripped the top of her thighs and spread her legs even wider so he could see her wet folds amongst her blond curls. Not giving her a chance to even think, let alone protest, he licked her up like the sweetest piece of candy.

"Nolan!" she shrieked.

He laughed to himself.

Now that that shock's out of the way, it's time to really enjoy myself.

He parted her pretty pink folds with his thumbs and admired her glistening flesh, especially her aroused clit.

Ah, my girl's going to love this.

He bent his head then licked, stroked, and nuzzled her sex, luxuriating in the very essence of Maggie. She tried to rise to his tongue's forays, but his grip held her down.

"Nolan," she whined.

"More, Baby?" he whispered.

"Yes!" she moaned.

He delved deep as his thumb raised the hood of her clit, and then he sucked as he pressed one finger deep inside her channel. He heard her gasp and relaxed when he realized it was a gasp of pleasure. He stroked in and out as he sucked her clit even harder, then he grazed it with his teeth and she shrieked out his name again and again as her body clenched hard around his finger. He felt pulse after pulse of her release coat his tongue and he savored every drop.

When she finally relaxed back down onto the bed he got up and picked up the condom he'd left on the nightstand.

"Oh yes, I want you to make love all the way with me now. I so want it," she said as she reached out to touch his sheathed cock.

Nolan shuddered and grabbed her hand to kiss it before she could touch him. If she did touch him, he wasn't sure how long he'd last, and he needed to make this good for her.

He knelt between her thighs and positioned himself at her entrance, watching her carefully. She stared up at him as he eased forward.

Her hot tight depths clutched him. He saw a frown begin to form, and he moved one hand until it rested above her mound. His thumb brushed through her wet curls and found its engorged target. He began circling the bud.

"Nolan," she panted.

"I'm here."

"I noticed." Inexorably, he moved deeper until he felt her virgin barrier. He hesitated, but she was having none of it.

"Don't stop, it feels too good."

He kept the pressure on her with his thumb, circling and swirling, listening to her breath break. When he was sure she was ready, he pressed through, going deeper, and she moaned with pleasure.

"Yes," she sighed.

He would have laughed except he was gritting his teeth, intent on going slow, on showing her the possibilities. He lifted his thumb up and she moved upwards to follow, sheathing him deeper. His thumb fluttered against her, teasing her—teaching her—until she moved up and down in a tempo that made sweat bead on his brow.

"Feels so good." She reached down and grasped his flanks, pulling him closer, deeper. Her heels rode up his body. She was ready.

Nolan pulled out and slid back in, savoring her sighs. Soon they found the perfect rhythm, and his moans of need melded with her soft sounds of pleasure.

He touched his forehead to hers. Their eyes met, unveiling all they were to one another.

It was as if they were blending their souls together. His arms reached around and hugged her close as they soared ever upwards, reaching for the stars, crying out each other's names.

CHAPTER SIXTEEN

She felt like a different person. She was no longer Margaret Celeste Rhodes, she was someone entirely different. *And no, it's not Mary Smith*, she thought with a grin as she quietly pulled out a can of Orange Crush and the half piece of chocolate cake that was left over in the mini-fridge.

Maggie couldn't believe how hungry she was.

That's what happens when you're a sex goddess. She grinned to herself. She carefully popped the top of her pop, praying she wouldn't wake either Nolan or Iris; both of them needed their sleep. Nolan, silly boy that he was, was under the impression that she and Iris were going to stay in this suite when he went back to Virginia to talk to his boss. That *so* wasn't happening. He did not need to be spending his hard-earned money on fancy hotel rooms when there was a perfectly good trailer for her and Iris to go back to.

What she couldn't stand was the idea of him having to leave. He said it was just going to be for a few days to talk to his boss about taking an official leave of absence. He said it would be fine, but Maggie was worried. What happened if his boss said no?

She put down the cake. She wasn't hungry anymore when she thought about Titus. Would he tell his friend at CPS that she was living in her poopy little trailer while Nolan was gone, and take Iris away? She wrapped her arms around her waist.

Then she heard a cry from her bedroom and she got up from the couch.

"Saved by the baby. That means no more worrying."

She opened the bedroom door and then closed it so Nolan wouldn't be disturbed. "What's going on, Sweet Pea? Is it diaper, hunger, or do you need a cuddle?"

When she leaned over the crib she saw the little pink bear that Bella had given Iris.

I can go to Trenda's!

"You're a dad," Kostya Barona grinned. "Congratulations!"

"He's a big brother," Gideon corrected. He had a big ole smile on his face too. "Congratulations, man. Do you have pictures? Please say she doesn't look like you."

Nolan pulled out his phone and scrolled through

until he got video of Bella and Maggie trying to get Iris to sit up.

"Fuck, that's cute. Look at that red hair," Gideon cooed.

"I want to see," Kostya demanded as he held out his hand for the phone. Nolan was laughing at the way Gideon had gone all mushy.

"Damn, the baby has your eyes, O'Rourke," Kostya said. "Who's the kid?"

"Believe it or not, that's Drake Avery's niece."

There was a knock on the doorjamb of Kostya's open office door. "Got a minute, Lieutenant?" Ryker McQueen asked. He was with Lincoln Hart and Jase Drakos.

"Do you need privacy?" Kostya asked.

"Nah, we'll be quick," Linc answered.

"So, what's up?" Kostya asked.

"Night Storm is wanting to do a joint training exercise, specializing in tracking."

"Max hasn't called me." Kostya frowned.

"Yeah, well, his kid and his wife have the flu so he has his hands full. Raiden mentioned it to Jase. Anyway, Kane's going to be calling you, and he deserves comeuppance for the shit he pulled while Gideon was in Oregon."

Gideon snickered.

"Quit your laughing," Kostya demanded. "It was your idea to begin with."

"What do you have in mind?" Kostya asked his men.

"Raiden knew we wanted to do something to Kane," Jase answered. "Since he and I are the trackers on both our teams, we think we can get Kane turned around enough that he'll be lost for at least forty-eight hours, and we'll take bets."

"So the rest of Night Storm is good with this?"

"Yep," Ryker answered Kostya.

"Go for it."

Nolan would have laughed, but he was still too bogged down with the Iris and Maggie issue.

"Thanks, Lieutenant," Jase smiled before the three of them left.

"What else is going on?" Kostya asked as he handed Nolan back his phone.

"It's complicated as fuck, and somebody needs a lesson."

"I'm listening."

"So am I," Gideon said as he got up and closed Kostya's office door.

"My mother knew she was in bad shape as she was close to giving birth to Iris. It was a high-risk pregnancy from the word go because of her age, and it just got worse and worse, but she never once considered ending it."

"I'm so sorry," Gideon breathed out.

Nolan nodded, "Yeah."

"Anyway, because she knew the risks, she left a will stating that Maggie would be the guardian of the baby if anything should happen to her. Maggie agreed, even though she had every intention of finding me and handing her over to me."

"She looked pretty attached to the baby," Kostya noted.

"Yeah, but she's on the run. Currently, she's known as Mary Smith, and that's what the guardianship is under. She's been on the run for two and a half years. There's this psychopath out after her that her father said she has to marry. He actually cut her up, and her dad still said she had to marry him."

"What?" Kostya bellowed.

"Exactly," Nolan gritted out. "I'm going to need Gideon's help to find out all about this isolated, backward community in bumfuck Minnesota that's off the grid that seems pretty cultish to me. Then I've got to track down this motherfucker Kyle and explain to him why it is endangering his health to keep following Maggie."

"Just how violent is this conversation going to be?" Kostya asked. "Just asking so I know how strong your alibi is going to need to be."

"He beat up this woman who helped house Maggie for two months, then almost killed a man who was her employer out in Arizona. He's escalating. Maggie assures me that her trail runs cold in Oklahoma, but I'm not so sure." He turned to look directly at Gideon. "She gave me the secure e-mail address that her brother created for her. Kyle sent her an article about the Arizona rancher who was injured. That means that

Kyle has a bead on her. I'm hoping you can trace it back to him."

"Of course I can," Gideon said.

"You two get on this. As for the time off you need to get things sorted for you and your baby sister. You take all the time you need, Nolan," Kostya said. "If you need any testimony to CPS or backup while you're in Tennessee, just holler."

"I will."

He and Gideon got up and left the office.

Maggie was glad that Trenda had been able to watch Iris today. It meant that she could come to the library alone and have the WeChat with Brian without having to worry about Iris making a fuss. She really didn't want Iris to pick up on her emotions if she found another upsetting e-mail from Kyle.

Nolan had told her not to check her e-mail anymore. He said that from now on his friend Gideon would monitor it for her, but she just couldn't do it. What happened if Jake or Carla or Jenny Cooper tried to get ahold of her? She needed to be able to read what they said.

She heard her WeChat ping.

Maggie: *I'm so glad to talk to you today, so much has happened since last Monday.*

Brian: *I have news for you too.*

Maggie: *Me first.*

Brian: *Okay*

Maggie: *Nolan O'Rourke came back. He's wonderful. More than wonderful. He couldn't be any better. He adores Iris and he went back to Virginia to talk to his boss today to figure out how he can arrange his time to care for Iris full time.*

Brian: *That is good news. Now you can leave.*

Maggie hunched over the library desk and moved closer to the computer, holding her stomach as it churned.

Maggie: *I can't leave yet. I have to work with Nolan to change the custody papers from me to him.*

Brian: *You don't have time for that. According to Laurel, the VanWycks have all already left. They're on their way to get you.*

Maggie: *Did she say where they're going?*

Brian: *South.*

Maggie: *Every place in America is south from Minnesota.*

Brian: *I couldn't stand it if anything happened to you. Please listen to me.*

Maggie: *Nolan is a SEAL, he'll protect me. Brian, I need you to find out where they're going. I think they're going to Oklahoma, and they won't find anything. Please ask Laurel to find out, if she can do it safely.*

Brian: *I'll call you tomorrow, okay?*

Maggie: *Same time?*
Brian: *Yes.*

Maggie opened her e-mail and didn't find anything. She breathed a sigh of relief. She closed everything down and headed back to Trenda's house.

———

"Fuck, this motherfucker is sick. He's out of his fucking mind." Gideon shook his head in disgust.

Nolan looked at the four different pictures displayed on the screen. Gideon had saved them onto his hard drive.

"The good news, Nolan, is we can use these to prosecute him."

"That won't be happening," Nolan snarled. He looked again at the pictures of Maggie tied down to the motel bed, all bloody where the bastard had cut her up.

"You're sure that Maggie won't have seen them?" Nolan asked again.

"Positive. She hadn't accessed her e-mail by the time I grabbed these. She's accessed it now, but all she found was an empty inbox."

"How about tracing his e-mail back to him?" Nolan asked

"That's a little trickier."

"What are you talking about? He's some rube from the dark ages."

Gideon rubbed the top of his head as he looked at his computer screen. "I agree with you. He is. I think that's the problem. He's made this simple. He's created a local Arizona cable e-mail account for the e-mail he sent to Maggie about that rancher Jake. He created it while he was in Arizona. He did it while he was in a library, sent the article, then shut the account down."

"What about this e-mail that he sent yesterday?"

"Another small cable company, this one in Oklahoma."

"Shit."

"What?"

"That was the next place Maggie was, after Arizona. How in the hell does he keep tracking her?" Nolan got up from the chair in Gideon's office and started pacing around. "We need more information. According to Maggie, her twin brother has an inside source into that fucking cult. We need to get in touch with him."

"Tell me about him," Gideon coaxed.

"His name is Brian. He's the one who set up the e-mail account. He WeChats with Maggie every Monday."

"He set up the account, did he?"

"Oh yeah, he's an online friend of this woman Carla Lester that Maggie stayed with in Idaho, and he also arranges for all of Maggie's burner phones."

Gideon grinned.

"Why don't you go help yourself to something in my fridge? This will take about a half hour, but I've got an idea."

———

"Are you ever going to tell me who you are and why you're running?"

Maggie looked up from the banana nut muffin that she'd been breaking up into tiny little crumbles. Trenda was sitting across from her at her pretty dining room table, giving her a welcoming smile.

Maggie took a deep breath. She really didn't want to offend Trenda, but before she could start, the older woman held up her hands.

"Trust me, Maggie, I know what it's like to have secrets. I've held mine close to my chest and haven't even told any of my family members. But I think you're ready, and I only want to help."

Maggie gave Trenda a wry smile. "Well, it sounds like you already know one of them, the fact that my name is Maggie."

Trenda nodded.

"I have a man kind of stalking me, but not in the real sense of the word. He's got my family's permission to pursue me."

Trenda frowned. "Can you explain that to me?"

"Where I come from, in my small, isolated town up in Minnesota, the men have absolute control. My father has chosen to marry me off to a psychopath, and I ran.

The first time my supposed fiancé caught me, he carved his initial into my ribs. I ran again, and so far he hasn't found me, but he's hurt the people that have helped me along the way."

Trenda nodded slowly. "I get it now. Let me guess —you want to run again."

"That's what my gut is telling me, but my heart is telling me something else."

"Your heart isn't just telling you to stay for Iris, is it?"

Maggie looked down at the destroyed muffin and shook her head. "How can I care this much for Nolan after so few days?"

"I'm just happy your heart is leading you in the right direction. Sometimes it doesn't, especially when you're young."

Maggie looked up and laughed. "Is that the voice of experience?"

"Yeah. Young, in love, and stupid is not a good combination. You're twenty, right?" Trenda asked.

"Twenty-one."

"Still, you're pretty young to have your head screwed on so straight."

"I kind of have to after all I've been through."

"Want to tell Auntie Trenda all about it?"

Maggie laughed. "How old are you?"

"Twenty-nine, and I'm now old, but when I got pregnant with Bella, I was way, way, young," she laughed. "And that was when I was twenty-two. That's why I figured you were young too."

"I'm young in age, not in spirit," Maggie answered, then she sighed. "So what do you want to know?"

"Before we get to your background, tell me about you and Nolan."

"I would love to talk to you about us. Oh my God, I don't know what to think. I'm all mixed up about him. Is it just because he's the first good man I've met?" Maggie got up from the table and started pacing. "I thought that might be it, but it isn't. Jake Sanders, my boss in Arizona, he was a really good man too, but we didn't have that spark, you know?" She looked over her shoulder at Trenda who nodded.

"And it's more than just a spark. It's a conflagration with Nolan. Oh heck, Trenda, I don't just think he's the best man I ever met, I think he's the best *person* I ever met. He tries so hard to do the right things in life, and the fact that he is willing to put his life on the line for our country? Who does that? Then there's the way he is with Iris. It's beautiful. You've seen that, right?"

Trenda nodded.

"And he's so good to me. But he's not perfect either, and that's good, because I wouldn't want someone who was a paragon, you know?"

She looked over at Trenda again, who was biting her lip. But Trenda nodded.

"He has a temper, but never at me, and never at Iris. You should have seen him when Arlo and Titus were trying to hurt me, I mean... Oh my goodness, I thought he would rip them apart, and that was all kinds of well... all kinds of hot. That's wrong that I thought that, wasn't it? It was. I shouldn't have thought that, should I have?"

She looked over at Trenda who was looking down at her lap and twisting her hands together, letting her hair cover her face. Trenda let out a cough, then Maggie continued.

"Do you know what he looks like in his t-shirts?! And then I saw him without his t-shirt, and it was crazy good. I mean, I couldn't stop staring at him. And then when I took off my sweater and he saw my scar, it didn't even matter to him, he still thought I was beautiful. Who thinks like that? I never thought I could feel so good, but he made everything feel wonderful."

Maggie sat back down in her chair, her muffin forgotten. She slammed her elbows on the table and looked at Trenda.

"So that's where I am with Nolan. I think maybe I love him, but I'm not sure. What do you think?"

Trenda looked up and Maggie saw the tears in her eyes—right before she burst out laughing.

"What are you laughing about?" Maggie asked indignantly.

"Remember when you said you weren't young?"

"Yeah," Maggie slowly agreed.

"Well, you are. If you haven't figured out that you're head over heels in love with Nolan O'Rourke you are young, naïve, and stupid," Trenda laughed.

"Am *not*," Maggie shouted. Then she clamped her hand over her mouth, worried she might have woken Iris.

Her eyes went wide as she thought over everything she just said. "Oh my goodness. I *am* young, naïve, and stupid. I'm totally gone for Nolan." She moaned. "I can't be gone for him. I'm on the run from a psychopath. I'm the last thing Nolan needs."

"Are you kidding? You're *just* the woman Nolan needs. You're perfect," Trenda grinned.

CHAPTER SEVENTEEN

"Here," Gideon said as he handed Nolan a satellite phone.

"Who's this?" Nolan asked as he put down his roast beef sandwich.

"Brian Rhodes. Your girlfriend, Margaret Rhodes' twin brother."

Nolan wiped his hands off on a paper towel, then took the satellite phone from Gideon's hand.

"Hello?"

"That guy says you're Nolan O'Rourke. How can I be sure?" a man asked.

"I know that your sister has long hair that is normally blond. I know that she has four brothers, Peter, Paul, Matthew, and you, and two sisters— Catherine and Ruth. I know Catherine has a little boy, and I know that some sick fuck named Kyle carved his initial into Maggie."

"That's an awful lot to know in such a short amount of time," Brian said.

"Well, Brian, I don't know what to tell you, except us chit-chatting isn't going to help your sister, now is it?"

Nolan had the phone up to his ear and Gideon motioned for him to put it on speaker, so he did.

"Brian, my teammate Gideon got ahold of you so we could work together. We need to know everything you do, to find out how to stop Kyle from coming after your sister."

"It's worse than you think," Brian said. "Not only is Kyle coming after her, his father and two brothers have joined him."

"Fuck! Just what kind of place do y'all come from?" Nolan demanded to know.

"A fucked up one," Brian admitted. "Kyle has tracked down Maggie as far as Oklahoma, and I don't know how he managed to do it. I really don't. She got the job using her burner phone and e-mails."

"It was the e-mails," Gideon interrupted. "And that's how we're going to stop him. I've gone through all of her e-mails since she's been in Jasper Creek. She's mentioned Tennessee, Trenda—but only by her first name—and Nolan O'Rourke. She's also mentioned the names Ginger and Iris—again, no last names. But I'm afraid now that Nolan has shown up in Jasper Creek that he'll be able to pinpoint her location."

"We need to get her out of there," Nolan snarled. "I'm going back on the first flight out."

"Would you hold on?" Gideon said as he grabbed Nolan's arm. "We need to figure out where Kyle is. Do you know anything, Brian?"

"I know that the VanWyck family left last night, but they're going by car. For the most part, nobody from Elk Bay likes airplanes. They require too much ID."

Nolan watched as Gideon checked something on his phone. "If they drive straight through, it's only twenty hours," Gideon announced. "They'll still have to figure out where Maggie is, though."

"They won't just go into town," Brian said. "They'll creep around on the edges. They're going to want to find her, then capture her and drag her home."

"Over my dead body."

"We're going to have to find them first," Gideon cautioned Nolan. "How heavily armed are they going to be?" he asked Brian.

"Over the past few years a lot of the council members have been gathering more and more guns, I think that includes some automatic weapons. I only know this because my brother Peter let it slip about an AK-47."

"Okay, I'm getting my ass back down there," Nolan said. "Brian, can you work to get us more intel?"

"I'm going to go back there. I can't handle asking Laurel to continue giving me information. It's too dangerous for her. I want to be there to protect her."

"What will happen to you?" Gideon asked.

"I'll be under suspicion, but to save face, my father

will allow me back in our home. He'll beat the hell out of me, but that's nothing new."

Gideon and Nolan looked at one another in confusion.

"He doesn't do it with his fists," Brian said, guessing their confusion. "He's a big, spare the rod, spoil the child, kind of man. He has a big stick that he used to whale on all of us growing up. He'll use that. I'll just have to take it. Like I said, nothing new. As long as he doesn't break any bones, I'll be able to protect Laurel."

"It sounds like that entire town of yours needs to be taken down," Nolan said.

"My brother Matthew and I are working on it," Brian said. "You'll keep me informed of what's going on?" he asked.

"Yep, and the same goes, right?" Nolan asked.

"You got it."

Brian hung up.

"That place is fucked up," Gideon said. "And you're saying your girl has her head on straight?"

"Gideon, she is one of the most put-together women I know. I don't know how in the hell that happened, but she is. She's made me see things and think of things in a whole new way. I've never felt better in my life."

"I can tell a difference, Nolan. You're not as closed off."

"It's because of her. There wouldn't have been a chance in hell that I could have believed I would be a good big brother—"

"Dad," Gideon interrupted.

"Okay, dad. Because of Maggie, I believe I can be a good dad to Iris. I actually believe it with my whole heart that I can do right by that little girl, and Maggie is the person that helped me to see that."

Gideon gave him a long assessing look, then he smiled. "I'm happy for you."

"So am I."

"And Maggie?"

"What about Maggie?"

"How do you feel about her?"

"That's easy. She's mine. She might not realize it yet, but she belongs to me, just like Iris does. Eight days ago I would have told you I wasn't good enough for someone. I couldn't ever be what a woman needed me to be."

"Bullshit," Gideon coughed into his elbow.

Nolan grinned. "Just telling you how I used to feel. You're all loved up with Judu now, you do feelings, right?"

"Don't get mushy with me, O'Rourke. I'm having to listen to Ryker all the time right now. If you go soft, that's going to leave me with Drakos. Don't do this to me, man," Gideon whined.

Nolan laughed. "I'm just saying that I remembered some things, and figured out some things while I was home, and Maggie helped me. I'm in love with her. I'm keeping her. She's mine."

"Now there's my boy. I approve of that. I'm liking

that caveman talk. I can get into that. No mush, more caveman."

Nolan laughed harder. "Let's book my tickets to Jasper Creek."

———

When he was at the Atlanta airport, Nolan had just enough time to stop at the USO before his connection to Knoxville.

"Mr. O'Rourke," Blessing called out to him before he even had a chance to walk over the threshold. He couldn't help the smile that crossed his face. She came around the counter and held out both hands, and he clasped them.

"How are you, Mizz Blessing?" he asked.

"I'm doing much better now that you're here," she said. She held her cheek up and he gave her a kiss.

"Tell me about the girls. I'm thinking things still aren't settled, am I right?"

Nolan shook his head ruefully. Well, she sure as hell wasn't a kook, that was for damn sure. "Would you like to see a video?" he asked.

"I would love to." Her smile got even bigger.

He pulled out his phone and showed her the same video that he'd shown Kostya and Gideon.

"Your sister has your eyes," she exclaimed midway through the video.

"You know, Mizz Blessing, most everybody who's

going to see that little girl is going to assume she's my daughter."

"People do a lot of assuming don't they?" she chuckled. "Now tell me who the other two beauties are."

"This is Bella Avery. She's six and she charges me a dollar every time I swear."

Blessing's eyes twinkled. "Delightful." Then her finger pointed to Maggie. "And this lady who holds your heart? What's her name?"

"Maggie."

"She's beautiful. I'm going to say the same thing I said last time, Nolan—they're lucky to have you."

"I hope you're right. But I'm worried."

"Of course you are. You wouldn't be the man you are if you weren't. But a bit of advice?"

"I would welcome it." He looked down at this mystical woman and waited with bated breath to hear what she would have to say.

"Never assume it's over until everything from your past is resolved."

"Okay," Nolan said slowly. "But begging your pardon, ma'am, that doesn't make a whole lot of sense."

"My dear boy, if things were just spelled out for us, then what fun would life be? Now check your watch; I think you're cutting it really close to catch your plane."

Nolan glanced down at his watch.

"Aw, shit, you're right." He turned and headed for the door.

"I think you owe Bella a dollar," Blessing called out after him.

———

"Where are you?" Nolan barked the question into his phone.

"Nolan?" Maggie asked tentatively. "Why are you angry at me?"

Reel it back.

"Sorry, Maggie. I just got worried for a moment when I got to the hotel and you'd checked out, and then I came here to the trailer and you weren't here either."

"You're back!" she exclaimed. "That's wonderful! I didn't think you'd be back so soon. Brian told me you talked to him, but he didn't mention you were coming back to Jasper Creek tonight."

"Honey, where are you?"

"I'm at Trenda's house."

Nolan pressed the bridge of his nose. "Why aren't you at the hotel like I asked?"

"Because it was silly to waste your money like that. But then I thought about Kyle maybe finding me at the trailer, or CPS coming to find me there or something, so I came to Trenda's house."

His head started to throb. "I can afford a hotel for a few days or for a few months, Honey."

"Nobody can afford a hotel room for a few months," Maggie laughed. "This was better. Anyway,

Bella likes playing with Iris. Come over. I want to see you. So does Iris."

At the thought of seeing Maggie and Iris, his mood soared. "I'll be there as soon as I can."

"That's good. Bye, bye." She hung up.

He looked over at the SUV that he'd rented and grimaced. No truck this time. He turned away from the front door and then looked back. Something wasn't right. Then he realized that even more slats were missing from the kitchen blinds than last time. He leaned over and peered inside.

"Goddammit," he whispered.

The inside of Maggie's trailer looked like a tornado had gone through it. Nolan pulled open the storm door, knowing it would be unlocked because Maggie had mentioned that the lock wasn't working on that, but his mouth filled with acid when he found the front door was unlocked as well. He pushed his way in and swore.

Somebody had been through the room with something like a bat. The small TV was smashed in and the couch and chairs were both upended. The changing table was smashed to pieces. None of the windows that he could see were broken, and that would have been on purpose, so as not to alert the neighbors. White powder was strewn all over the threadbare rug and linoleum. For a moment Nolan wondered what it was until he saw the bags of flour and sugar thrown from the pantry onto the kitchen floor. All of the dishes had been pulled out of the cabinets and tossed around the house. The only thing not broken were the plastic baby bottles, but even those had been stomped on.

Nolan couldn't tell if this was a crime of rage, or if someone was looking for something, but when he passed the bathroom and saw that it was untouched, he figured it was rage. He went to the small bedroom and found the crib thrown against the wall and broken. Maggie's mattress was shredded with a knife. The butterfly curtains had been ripped off the windows and shredded as well.

Yep, definitely rage.

Thank fuck Maggie and Iris had not been here.

Nolan took out his phone and called Gideon.

"What's up?" Gideon answered. "Shouldn't you be making time with your woman and tucking in Iris to bed?"

"Could the VanWycks be here already?" Nolan asked.

"Yeah, why?"

"I'm here in Maggie's trailer. It's been destroyed. She wasn't here, she took Iris to Trenda's house, but man, when I say destroyed, I mean destroyed. Her mattress was sliced to pieces with what I would have to guess was a hunting knife, all of her furniture was toppled, and almost everything else was smashed with what looks like a baseball bat. Jesus, Gideon, I can't even imagine what would have happened if she'd been here."

"Why did you ask if the VanWycks made it to

Jasper Creek? Were you thinking someone else did it?" Gideon asked.

"No, I just wondered if Kyle was acting on his own, or if he had his family helping him. How in the hell did Kyle all of a sudden track Maggie down to this trailer so fast? I was thinking that maybe someone from his family had helped him find her, is all."

"Gotcha. Well, yeah, the father and two brothers would have arrived six hours ago. The father went to Rainy River Community College at International Falls, and unlike his son, he actually graduated. His specialty was economics, so no computer. But, because he was economics, he's handling all the money for the community. That does mean he has to be savvy about computers these days, and savvy with the outside world. I would think that he might be able to find Maggie."

"Why isn't he reining his son in?"

"Who can get in the minds of these whack jobs? I'm coming down."

"You can't, you've got things to do," Nolan protested.

"Kostya gave me and some others blanket time off to come help you. We're taking it. You'll see us soon." Gideon hung up.

CHAPTER EIGHTEEN

How can a person feel both giddy and scared at the same time? Maggie wondered. This was darned ridiculous.

"I'm going to take Bella and Iris for a walk in the park," Trenda said innocently.

"You can't do that," Maggie wailed.

"But MaryMaggie, we want to go," Bella whined. She came over and grabbed Maggie's hand where she stood by the window. "Mama said that Nolan was coming back and you two needed adult time. I know what that means. You're going to kiss like Aunt Evie and Uncle Aiden, or Aunt Karen and Uncle Drake."

"When have you seen Evie and Aiden kiss? Have you been peeking in on them again? I told you that you'd get in trouble if I found out about that." Trenda sounded severe.

"It wasn't my fault I came into the kitchen and found them, Mama. I was surprised. I mean, Uncle

Drake is always kissing Aunt Karen, but I didn't know that Uncle Aiden kissed Aunt Evie."

Trenda laughed ruefully. She sidled up to Maggie. "My family," she said ruefully.

"I like your family. The men are really nice. They think it's funny when the women talk back to them. And they do that a lot."

"I can't imagine a world where Evie didn't give people shit," Trenda whispered.

"I heard that, Mama."

"We agreed, I get the ultimate pass because I clothe and feed you."

"I know. It's okay, I make enough from Uncle Drake and his friends."

"Go put your coat on, and put out Iris's warm bunny suit so I can put that on her. We need to go, Lovebug."

"Okay, Mama."

"I better get a move on so you two can kiss," Trenda teased.

Maggie didn't want to tell her friend how nervous she was. She hoped she could kiss, and much, much more.

Trenda left for the guest room so she could bundle up Iris. Maggie looked out the window. Where was he?

———

Nolan decided he was not going to tell Maggie about her trailer. He'd just keep her away from it until he talked her into moving to Virginia with him. As he pulled into the driveway, Trenda was pulling out. Bella was waving at him, so he waved back. He could see Iris in her car seat. He didn't wonder too much about where they were going, he was just happy he'd have some alone time with Maggie.

He wanted to see her safe and happy.

"Where's your truck?" she asked as she opened the door for him.

"They were out of them at the rental agency."

She looked nervous.

"Are you going to invite me in?"

"Oh. Oh yeah." She moved to the side and waved him inside.

As soon as he walked down the hall, his gaze immediately focused in on the couch that she fell asleep on, then he thought about the guest bedroom where he'd undone her camisole. Yeah, this would always be a good house for him.

"Are you hungry? Trenda and I went shopping—"

He pulled her into his arms and swooped in for a kiss. Immediately, he realized her lips felt different, tasted different. He paused for a moment, trying to figure it out. He brought his hands up and cupped her cheeks, and then he realized what it was—it was the emotion behind the kiss. Before, she had been so open and welcoming, but now she felt tentative and shy. It didn't make sense, but it didn't matter, he could work with it. He slowly coaxed her to open her mouth and when he did—when passion flared—he felt he'd climbed the highest mountain.

Slowly he pulled back. "I am hungry," he admitted. "But not for food."

She blushed. "Oh."

He stroked the back of his knuckles against the hot skin of her cheek.

"What is it, Maggie? You seem shy."

"I feel shy," she admitted. "I don't know why. It doesn't make any sense. I figured some things out about you. How I feel about you. And it's too soon."

Her eyes were darker than normal. He saw the passion, but he saw conflict as well. "What's too soon, Honey?"

"I'm pretty sure I'm in love with you."

Nolan wrapped her in a tight hug, treasuring her, as his heart exploded. Then he replayed her words.

"*Pretty* sure?"

"Almost sure. I've never been in love before, so how would I know?"

He bent low, then touched his forehead to hers. "Sometimes you just know. It's instinct. I feel like the world revolves around you. I think about you all the time. I have to—and I mean, *have* to—protect you. When I'm away from you, it feels like I've left half of my heart with you. I feel like you belong to me."

She stiffened.

"But Maggie, not in the way you grew up with. I feel like we're parts of the same soul, like we were meant to be together. I agree it doesn't make a lick of sense since we just met, but I want what's best for you, and that's anything you want. I don't want to control you, I want to see you fly."

Her eyes flared. He felt the spark go from her to him, then back again, like a continuous loop of electricity, of love.

"You love me?"

"Love isn't a big enough word to describe how I feel. I don't know how it happened, but you burrowed into my heart." Nolan stood up straight and she leaned her head back to look at him. He stared off into the distance. "No, I don't think that's right either. You opened up my heart and brought in the light and love, you expanded me to be a better man."

He looked back down at her, then bent to give her the most reverent kiss imaginable.

When he stood back up he saw a tear dripping down her face, but he wasn't worried. Maggie was happy.

Cherished. Loved. She felt like she had flown to the moon and back. She slid her hands up his chest and clasped his neck. "I love you too. So much. I can't even begin to describe it."

She chuckled. "But we can't. Trenda just took the girls to the park, so we don't have time."

"Dammit."

"But there is food in the fridge, so I can feed you..."

"I guess that will have to do."

He pulled her hands off his neck, then tangled his fingers with her so she could guide him to the kitchen. "Do you like mustard in your potato salad?"

"I'm up for anything," he replied.

"It's really good. How about a ham and Swiss sandwich? I'll toast it."

"Now you're talking," he squeezed her hand.

"I'm hoping you can talk while I put together your lunch. Did you get the time off? Will the Navy be able to help expedite transferring my guardianship to you?"

Maggie went to the fridge and got out everything she was going to need to feed this big man. "Are you really hungry? Are you going to want one sandwich, or two?"

"We'll start with one. And yeah, I got the time off; that was easy."

"That's wonderful." She looked up at him from the tomato that she was slicing. "How come I hear a but?"

"Gideon was able to track down Brian. I had a conversation with him. So your name is Maggie Rhodes, huh?"

Maggie giggled. "It's actually Margaret Celeste Rhodes, if we want to be exact. How did you end up talking with Brian? Was it that friend Gideon who figured out how to do it?"

"Yep. Your brother is very protective of you."

"Yeah, he is. He's my twin."

Maggie paused. "But that's not the but. Something's wrong. Kyle is in Jasper Creek, isn't he?"

"Yeah. He's found out where you live. He's found

the trailer. We need to get you someplace safe."

"How do you know he's found out where I live?"

"The front door was unlocked. You would have locked it, right?"

Maggie wrapped her arms around her stomach and nodded. "Did he do anything? Did he take anything?"

"It's all right, Maggie. Right now I just need to figure out a place that's safe for you to stay, okay?"

The front door opened.

"We're home," Bella shouted out.

Maggie looked at her. Had it really been that long?

"Not so loud, Lovebug, you'll wake Iris."

"Give her to me," Nolan said as he made his way to Trenda. She handed over the baby and Nolan immediately pulled her into his arms. He touched her cheek with his forefinger.

Maggie loved watching their interaction.

"She's out like a light. I think she needs her bed," Trenda said.

"I'll put her in her crib," Nolan said as he headed to the guest room.

Trenda rushed to the kitchen. "How'd it go?"

"It couldn't have gone better," Maggie said with a dreamy smile.

"I'm so happy," her friend said as she gave her a hug.

Nolan came back to the kitchen.

"I just put your sandwich in the oven," Maggie said. "It'll be ready in a minute."

"Okay. Trenda," Nolan said. "We've got a

problem."

"Just one?" she asked sarcastically. "Hold on while I set Bella up with some coloring."

"Mama, I don't want to color, I want to know what the problem is," Bella whined.

"You're going to listen to your mother, go to your room, and color in your butterfly coloring book that Maggie gave you."

"Is your name Mary or Maggie?" Bella asked. "Or is it MaryMaggie?"

"Maggie," Maggie answered. "I needed to hide for a little while, so I used a pretend name. My real name is Maggie."

The little girl frowned, then smiled. "Good, I like Maggie better. Thank you for my coloring book. I'll color a real pretty butterfly for you." She ran to her bedroom.

"Okay, before you start, Nolan, let me tell you what I've done," Trenda requested.

"Go for it."

"I contacted Alice." At his confused look, she clarified. "The sheriff. Anyway, Arlo showed up at the hospital in Gatlinburg. He had to have surgery. He swears that his arm was broken by Nolan O'Rourke. I asked Alice when, then explained you were over at my house playing gin rummy at the time, so it couldn't have been you."

"It's kind of a flimsy alibi since people saw me at Rowdy's," Nolan pointed out.

Maggie and Trenda laughed.

"What?" Nolan asked.

"Everybody hates Arlo, and nobody at Rowdy's ever talks to the cops," Maggie explained. "Alice is stuck with your alibi."

"That's good. What about Titus and his development?" Nolan asked.

"I'm leaving that up to the town council," Trenda said. "Right now Alice doesn't have anything to charge Titus with because Arlo isn't talking, but the council will be pretty interested to hear that Titus is behind the land buyouts."

Maggie saw Nolan's satisfied grin.

"Trenda, do you know any place that you, your daughter, Maggie, and Iris can lay low for a while?"

"Not really, why? Why can't we stay here? Are we lying low from the man who is stalking Maggie?"

Uh-oh. Nolan was rubbing the back of his neck, not a good sign.

"Trenda, it's known around town that you babysit Iris."

"Nobody would tell a stranger that information," Trenda said vehemently.

"Not willingly, no."

Maggie gasped.

"Are you thinking this man might hurt someone to get information about Maggie? I need to call Alice."

"I think that's a good idea. I want her people on the lookout for strangers. In the meantime, I want the four of you hidden. Someplace where they wouldn't think of finding you."

Trenda bit her lip. "You're going to say someplace defensible, aren't you?"

"What are you talking about?" Maggie asked.

CHAPTER NINETEEN

God love the sister of a SEAL. Nolan grinned.

"You're absolutely right, I want defensible."

"Why not just leave town?" Maggie asked.

"It's too late, they're here."

"What do you mean they're here," Trenda demanded to know.

"They already broke into Maggie's trailer," Nolan explained.

Trenda didn't say anything, her eyes just got wide. She pulled her phone out of the back of her jeans pocket and pressed a number that was clearly on speed dial. She set her phone down on the counter and put it on speaker.

After just two rings, a man answered. "How's my beautiful baby sister?"

"Don't have time for that, Drake. We've got a sitch."

"How bad? Which sister?"

"Kind of me. I've got Nolan O'Rourke, Navy SEAL standing beside me."

"What team?" Drake barked. "Tell me the situation right now, O'Rourke."

"Omega Sky, out of Little Creek."

"And?"

"Trenda is involved because she's been babysitting for a woman who has a madman after her. He's tracked down the woman's trailer and annihilated it. His father and two brothers are very likely in town."

Maggie gasped. Nolan didn't look up.

"We're all at Trenda's house. Need to move now. Need somewhere unknown and defensible. Got any ideas?"

"What do you mean—" Drake stopped himself. "Trenda, go to Evie and Aiden's place. You have the keys and the code for the alarm. I'll get the code for the gun safe, and it better not be biometric, or I'll shoot that motherfucker Aiden."

"Defensible?" Nolan asked.

"Aiden used to be second in command of Black Dawn. He's a paranoid fuck, damn right it's defensible."

Nolan breathed a sigh of relief. "I'm assuming it's not under the name Avery?"

"Nope, O'Malley."

"I'll call you when we get there and explain everything," Nolan promised.

"I might be on a flight by then."

Nolan snorted. "You can't rustle up a plane that fast."

"Watch me."

Iris wouldn't stop crying. It was as if she could feel the tension in the air. Evie and Aiden's house was beautiful, but Maggie didn't care one single darn, not as soon as she saw all the guns, and bigger guns, and machine guns that Nolan got out of Aiden's gun safe. It didn't bother Trenda at all and thank God Bella was way, way, way on the other side of the house playing video games on the biggest TV that Maggie had ever seen in her life.

Nolan had all of the guns spread out on the great room floor, and he had explained he was checking them. She didn't know for what. Trenda was pulling out ammunition from the gun safe and handing it over to Nolan.

"Okay Trenda, we're going to need to keep Bella isolated to one or two rooms. I want to put some of the rifles in strategic places so I can get to them quick when I need them. I plan to put them up high, out of her reach, but I want to be extra cautious."

"I'll move the video games to the master bedroom; that TV is pretty big too. I'll find a cooler and pack it with some of the stuff we bought at the grocery store on the way over."

Nolan nodded.

"Maggie, you're going to help me figure out where to put the ammunition after I've got the rifles in place."

She nodded.

"Is anyone answering their phones yet?" Maggie asked. It had taken them an hour to get here after they packed up what they needed from Trenda's, stopped at the grocery store, and made it here.

"No, I'm assuming they're all in the air."

"Why isn't the sheriff coming?" Maggie asked.

"Honey, Alice's hands are tied," Trenda answered. "So far all she has is the fact that your trailer has been vandalized. There have been no threats made. I have asked her for help, and she promised that patrol cars will drive by."

"But that won't help."

Trenda went over and hugged Maggie. "That's how stalker laws work, Sweetheart. I'm going to go get Bella and Iris situated in the master bedroom."

Maggie looked over at Nolan, who seemed relaxed as he opened up another rifle and looked down the long part that you shoot from. He smiled and put it down.

"Is that one good?" she asked.

"All of Aiden's shit is top of the line. When it comes to firepower, we're covered!"

"Do you really think all of this is necessary?" Maggie asked as she looked down at the floor. Nolan stood up from his crouch and stepped over the guns and rifles. He took Maggie into his arms.

"I'm so sorry, but yes I do. When I talked to your

brother, he told Gideon and me that he had seen the men in Elk Bay amassing weapons. Even AK-47s."

"What are those?"

Nolan pointed with his foot at the M4A1-Carbine. "It's like that rifle, there."

"That's a machine gun, isn't it?"

"It does fire a lot of rounds really fast," Noland admitted. "But it's not a machine gun."

Maggie felt herself breathing too fast, she needed to calm down. It was finally occurring to her that there might be an actual gunfight. How was this happening?

I can't breathe.

She gripped the front of Nolan's shirt.

I can't breathe.

She dug her nails into his chest.

I can't breathe.

Black dots were swimming before her eyes.

The next thing she knew, she was on a loveseat with her head between her knees and Nolan stroking her back. "Sip the air. Just one sip at a time, Baby. Just a little sip," he said as he rubbed circles on her back.

Maggie coughed, then tried to take in a breath.

It worked! I can breathe!

She tried to sit up, but Nolan pressed down on her gently. "Stay there for just a minute. I'm going to get you a glass of water. Keep taking deep breaths in, hold them, then blow them out slowly. Okay?"

"Okay," Maggie said hoarsely.

By the time Nolan was back with the water, she was under control. "I'm sorry," she said. He looked so concerned, and she hated that she was worrying him when everything else was so out of control.

"It's okay Maggie, I know this is a lot."

"It finally occurred to me that all of us could die."

She watched in shock as a beautiful smile crossed his face. "That's not going to happen. Don't you realize, all they want is to take you back home? They're not the type to kill you, or innocent women or children, now, are they?"

Maggie thought back to everything she knew about the VanWyck family. She had been over to their house for dinner on more than one occasion. She gave a sigh of relief. "You're right."

Then she clutched Nolan's hand. "But what about those machine guns?"

"That's to scare you, and possibly to take out somebody like me. I promise, Kyle's father and brothers aren't going to hurt you or the others. But it's my job to stop him from taking you, by any means necessary."

Maggie nodded. "I understand."

───────

Everybody was in the master suite when Gideon called him. "We'll be there in less than three hours," he said.

"Okay. Where are you?"

"We're on I-75. It's faster driving from Atlanta than waiting for the plane. Jase and Linc are driving one truck, me and Ryker are in another. What's going on?"

Nolan explained the situation with Aiden's house

and arsenal. "My problem is that we can't just have them spread out all over Jasper Creek, creating havoc. They need to be rounded up and taught a lesson."

"Agreed. You're absolutely sure that you can't be found where you're at?" Gideon asked.

"You're kidding, right? Nothing is ever a hundred percent, and I have contingency plans, but I think this place is secure."

"You got a plan?" Gideon asked.

"Yeah. Since they found Maggie's trailer, it won't be long before they find Trenda's place. I really want to capture them there."

"You're not leaving the women and children, are you?" Gideon asked incredulously.

"Fuck no. I was really hoping y'all might be here in time to set something up."

"I hope we are," Gideon said. "Now tell me that's not your only plan."

"Well..." Nolan started. "I was thinking that my brilliant friend who was able to get Brian Rhodes on the phone, has surely found a way to connect with Kyle VanWyck. Don't tell me you don't have his cell phone tracked."

Gideon chuckled. "As a matter of fact, I do. I was just waiting to hear what sorry-assed plan you had before I gave you your birthday present."

"So where is that piece of shit?"

"He's at someplace called the LeeHy Motel. It's—"

"You don't need to tell me, I know exactly where

the LeeHy is. I think half of Jasper Creek lost their virginity there."

"TMI, my friend, TMI."

"How long has he been there?" Nolan asked.

"He's been there since we left Virginia."

"Probably tired after trashing Maggie's trailer. I'd go get him, except I cannot leave the women and children," Nolan gritted out.

"Exactly right. We'll be there soon."

"Good. That way we can have some of you scooping up Kyle, and others at Trenda's to provide a surprise party to whichever other VanWycks show up."

"You do realize that Kyle could be with his family," Gideon pointed out.

"I don't care how it works out, I want that entire VanWyck family put on notice—Maggie is off limits."

"Agreed," Gideon said. "Agreed."

Maggie came out to the great room where Nolan was. She was carrying Iris. All of the guns were hidden somewhere. Well except for the two that Nolan had strapped to his sides in shoulder holsters.

"I thought you were going to stay in the master suite," Nolan said.

"I thought you could use a little Iris time," Maggie smiled. "She's up and playful."

She saw Nolan's eyes soften as he held out his arms.

"Nope. Got to get rid of the guns before you get to hold the baby."

Nolan pulled the guns out of the holsters and set them down on the side table, then Maggie deposited Iris into his arms. Iris immediately started smiling and kicking her legs.

"She missed you."

"Well, I missed her too." Nolan rubbed his nose against Iris's, who then tried to grab his. She chortled and Nolan laughed. He tickled her tummy. "Have you been a good girl for Mommy?"

Maggie bit back a gasp. "I'm not her Mommy," she protested.

"If you're not her Mommy, I don't know who is." Nolan looked up at her with his electric blue eyes, forcing her to believe what he was saying.

"It's too complicated," Maggie protested.

"We'll uncomplicate it. We'll get rid of this motherfucker and his whacked out family. You'll come to Virginia and live with me, and then you'll act surprised when I get down on my knees and give you a ring."

Thank God she wasn't still holding Iris, she probably would have dropped her.

"You can't be serious, we've only known each other for nine days."

"There is one thing I've learned being a SEAL and learning about my mother's life... do you know what that is?"

Maggie shook her head.

"Life's too fragile, and it's too fucking short. We never know what's around the next corner, and we have to grab hold of love when we can. That's what my mama did in the end, isn't it?"

Maggie nodded.

"What do you want, Maggie?"

"I want you. I never thought I would want to be married, but I really do love and trust you. I want to make a family with you and Iris."

He took two steps toward her, then wrapped his free arm around her so that he was holding both Maggie and Iris.

"Good to know that when I'm kneeling in front of you, you're not going to kick me to the curb," he grinned.

"Never."

CHAPTER TWENTY

Nolan hadn't realized just how scared he'd been until he saw the two trucks coming up Aiden's driveway and felt the boulder roll off his chest. Yeah, he'd been in some tight situations in his life, but he'd never had his woman and his child at risk before.

He chuckled when the red truck fishtailed. It had to be Jase driving. He went out to meet his friends.

They all came out with duffel bags that Nolan knew contained firepower.

"I want to see the kid," Ryker said before anyone else could talk. Nolan grinned. Ryker came from a big family out in California, and he was all about his nieces and nephews.

"Iris should be up from her nap in another hour. Then I'll let you change her diaper and everything," Nolan promised.

"I rock changing shitty diapers," Ryker exclaimed proudly.

Nolan rolled his eyes.

"Come inside and we can go over everything." He looked around the huge front yard once again and smiled. Aiden had done a great job making sure that there was a lawn perimeter three hundred and sixty degrees all around his house. Yep, he definitely made his house defensible.

"Who owns this again?" Jase asked as Nolan ushered them into the great room.

"Aiden and Evie O'Malley. Aiden is on the Midnight Delta team."

"Gideon, I want to be transferred to a California team, obviously they get paid a whole hell of a lot more than us peons in Virginia," Jase complained.

Linc hit Jase in the back of the head. "Hey, Einstein, he's probably like Gideon and made a zillion dollars working for a tech company before enlisting."

"I knew I should have paid attention during math class," Jase grumbled. He pulled out his M4A1-Carbine from his duffel bag. "So who we going to save, and who we going to maim?" he asked Nolan.

Trenda walked into the room. "Hello, gentlemen."

Nolan noticed Jase Drakos's eyes light up as he spotted the woman. "Trenda Avery, I'd like to introduce you to the members of my team," Nolan said.

She smiled and nodded.

"This is my second-in-command, Gideon Smith," Nolan said as he motioned to the formidable African American man.

"I've heard a lot about you." Trenda smiled. "Thanks for everything you've done so far."

"You're welcome."

"This next one who looks like he just walked off a California beach is Ryker McQueen." Ryker grinned and waved. "The third man who is currently putting on his holster is Lincoln Hart, he is our sniper."

"Why'd you tell her that?" Linc frowned. "Now she'll look at me weird."

"She was going to look at you weird no matter what," Jase spoke up. "My name is Jase Drakos. I track things down." He smiled and stepped forward to shake Trenda's hand. "Let me know if you ever lose anything."

Trenda laughed. "So you're that one in the crowd. There's always one. My brother is Drake Avery from the Midnight Delta team. Aiden O'Malley is my brother-in-law, so Jase, I've got your number. I want to thank all of you for getting here so quickly."

She looked over at Nolan. "Everybody else is napping. When I heard the trucks, I thought I could warm up the lasagna real quick, and feed everybody while you all brief one another."

"That's much appreciated, ma'am," Gideon smiled.

She pointed off to one side. "The dining room's through there. I'll bring out the food when it's ready."

"No you won't," Jase said. "Holler when it's ready, and I'll come get it. You don't need to be waiting on us."

Nolan shook his head and rolled his eyes again. Yep, Jase was in fine form, but wait until he met

Trenda's brother. Drake would shut this shit down in a heartbeat.

Nolan pulled out the few eight-and-a-half-by-eleven pieces of paper that he'd been drawing on, as well as the copies that he had made for the men, and passed them out.

"Okay, first, here are the players."

"I don't know all the names, but we have Kyle 'the psychopath' VanWyck. He's Maggie's stalker who has tried to kill people in the past. He's primed to kill. I think he's been here in Jasper Creek for at least twenty-four hours. He's currently at the LeeHy Motel, right, Gideon?"

Gideon looked down at the tablet he'd pulled out of his backpack. "Yep, he's still there."

"These are the other three. We've got daddy, and two brothers who just came down from Elk Bay to back up Kyle's play to bring Maggie back so she can marry Kyle."

"What the fuck? That's whacked," Jase said. "What kind of place is Elk Bay? Where is it?"

"It's an isolated town in Minnesota, close to Canada. For our purposes, just consider it a cult. Anyway, they got here, probably within the last eight to twelve hours. I would assume they've hooked up with Kyle, but he could be operating on his own. Hard to tell."

"Why wouldn't he have hooked up with his family?" Linc asked.

"It's a gut feeling I have," Nolan answered. "The

way he trashed Maggie's trailer tells me he is off his rocker. He might not want to interact with his brothers, let alone his dad. I'm scared that he's too mad at Maggie to want her to just come home."

"You think he might just want to kill her?" Ryker asked.

Nolan looked around the dining room, making sure they were alone. "He's tortured her before, and I think he's escalated."

"Fuck," Jase breathed out. "Okay, we have to make sure that she's protected all the time, until Kyle is taken out."

"Agreed."

"So, what's this a map of?" Gideon asked as he looked at the other paper.

"This is a layout of the inside of Trenda's house. The other shows the outside with her neighbor's houses. I think that's where Kyle is going to go next. It's known that Maggie has Trenda babysit Iris."

"You want someone to sit on the house, and take him out?" Ryker asked.

"Because of the neighborhood, it's got to be done inside. So somebody has to be lying in wait. Preferably more than one, in case it's the family instead of Kyle."

Gideon nodded.

"Jase, come help me with the food," Trenda called out.

Nolan watched the taillights as the trucks drove down the driveway. He'd be hearing from the four men in about a half hour, so everything was good, but he still felt like he was missing something.

Before they'd left, all of them had had a chance to meet Iris, Maggie, and Bella. Bella had earned seventy dollars within ten minutes, forty of it from Jase. Maggie had watched in wonder as Ryker had expertly changed Iris's poopy diaper.

"You've got a couple of keepers," Gideon had whispered to Nolan as Ryker had gotten down on the baby blanket with Iris and Bella.

"I know it," Nolan agreed. "I'm going to marry her."

"Good for you," Gideon grinned. "I'm proud of you, O'Rourke."

That felt really good coming from the older man.

"Now, how do you feel about the plan?" Gideon asked Nolan for the first time.

"Feel?"

"Yeah, what is your gut saying?"

"Logically it seems like we're doing everything right, but I'm still worried we're missing something."

"I agree. If something goes south, Linc and I are going to haul ass back here."

"Shouldn't you go to Trenda's?"

"Nope. We're coming here."

Nolan nodded. He liked that plan.

But now here he was, waiting in the dark like a sitting duck.

Maggie was in Aiden and Evie's gorgeous bathroom washing her hands when her cell phone vibrated. She saw an Elk Bay area code and frowned. The only person she could think of that might be calling her from an Elk Bay number would be Brian, so she answered.

"Margaret?"

Her blood went cold. It was her brother Paul and he sounded angry. "Hello, Paul. How did you get this number?"

"You're foolish to think that when we cared enough to find you, that Father and I wouldn't be able to."

"Goodbye—"

A woman screamed from Paul's end of the line before she had a chance to hang up.

Catherine?

Ruth?

"Paul, stop it. Don't hurt her."

The screaming stopped. "I won't hurt Laurel, as long as you do what I tell you."

Laurel?

Brian's Laurel?

"Where are you?"

"I'm at Obadiah VanWyck's house, with Ronny Atwood, Laurel's intended. You know, the man she's going to marry at Christmas? The three of us were having a conversation when Father called me. He seems to think you're not at your friend's house. He needs you to go to that woman's restaurant so he can take you home."

"You're all out of your minds."

Another piercing cry came through the phone. "Please stop it," Laurel begged.

"You better get to Poppy's restaurant. Don't bring the brat. Don't bring anyone. I'd threaten Laurel's life, but that would be a lie. But I will tell you that she will suffer. She will suffer a great deal if you don't do as I say."

When the phone went dead Maggie stood with it still up to her ear. Then she looked at herself in the mirror and saw that she was crying. She didn't know what to do, but she couldn't let Laurel go through anything like she had suffered.

"The phone was here at the hotel, but not him," Gideon yelled over the line.

"Get back here right now. I've got an emergency," Nolan yelled back.

"On it," Gideon responded.

Nolan hung up. He looked around the great room wildly. He needed to stay focused, but the idea of Maggie in danger killed him.

Trenda came running into the room with her arm outstretched to hand him her phone. "It's Alice, she needs to talk to you."

Nolan took the phone.

"Hello," he said curtly, praying it was important.

"One of my deputies scooped up your friend Arlo tonight. He was drunk off his ass. He was talking about Mary Smith getting her just rewards. Said he knew that you'd be taken out too. Couldn't get much else out of him. How in the hell is Arlo involved with this stalking case?" the sheriff demanded to know.

"I don't know," Nolan said.

"Well, at least this is one chess piece off the board for the night."

"Yeah, there is that," Nolan breathed out. "But only a pawn. And a broken one at that."

Alice chuckled. "Gotta go."

Nolan handed Trenda back her phone. "How's everybody back in the master suite?"

"Maggie's got Iris and Bella calm and happy, I don't know how since she looks nervous as hell. What's going on?"

"Her father is here, and her brother is back home hurting a woman he cares about and telling her that if she doesn't turn herself over to her father, he'll hurt her a lot more."

"Oh, God."

"I need Gideon here, I can't leave you—"

"You two go. I'm more than competent with a gun, rifle and an M4A1-Carbine," Trenda insisted.

Nolan did nothing more than raise his eyebrow.

"But—" Trenda started.

"Do you really think I'm going to go for that? In your heart of hearts would you want me to?"

Trenda's shoulders drooped and she sighed. "No."

"It's not that you aren't capable, but you, Iris, and Bella are precious, and you know it."

"Bella and Iris are," Trenda said.

Nolan put his hand on Trenda's shoulder. "No, all three of you are precious."

CHAPTER TWENTY-ONE

Maggie squeezed Nolan's hand with both of hers.

Iris is safe.

Iris is safe.

"Honey, it's going to be all right."

Maggie took a deep breath, then smiled. "I just wish you could be meeting your future father-in-law under better circumstances."

Nolan burst out laughing.

"I love you, Margaret Celeste Rhodes."

He pulled up their hands and kissed her knuckles. "It's going to be all right, I promise you."

She turned around and looked out the back of the SUV. "I don't see Gideon's truck."

"You're not supposed to."

"Father's going to be angry that I brought you."

"Maggie, your father was going to be angry no matter what happened, now wasn't he?"

"He won't know I'm even there."

A block from the restaurant, Nolan pulled into the hardware store parking lot. "Call your father. Find out where he is."

"I don't know his phone number," she admitted.

"No problem." Nolan stroked her hair back from her forehead. "I can't wait to see you as a blonde." He pulled out his phone and pressed a number. "Gideon?"

He waited for Gideon to respond.

"Maggie doesn't know her father's number, can you get it for us?"

Nolan smiled at Maggie. "He's getting it."

"How?"

"Magic." He hung up the phone, then gave her a sexy smile. "I've heard about all of your other family. Tell me about your mother."

Maggie knew that he was asking just to take her mind off everything, but she answered anyway.

"She's sad all the time," Maggie said softly. "Even when Catherine had her son, Mother didn't smile. One day I would like to get her to leave, but I don't think she ever will. She doesn't know any other way. I remember her father, my Grandfather Abe. He was the same way as my father."

"How about when you were younger?"

Maggie thought back. "Well, she was the one who got me addicted to chocolate. Even though that was something we weren't supposed to have, she would always buy us treats when she'd go up to Canada, and my favorite was milk chocolate. But the very, very best was when she got me these chocolate bars with caramel. They were Cadbury. But Father found out when I was twelve. Mother got a beating, so it never happened again."

"Shit, Honey, I didn't want to bring up a bad memory."

Nolan's phone rang and he answered it. When he hung up, he took Maggie's phone and dialed a number, put it on speaker and put it on the center console.

"Hello, who's this?" The man sounded angry.

"It's me, Father, Maggie."

"Your name is Margaret."

Maggie just shook her head, trying not to get upset. "Where am I supposed to meet you?"

"At the restaurant," he shouted.

"Where at the restaurant? Inside? In the parking lot? Where, Father?"

"Don't you backtalk me!"

Maggie didn't reply.

"The far corner of the parking lot. I am in the family car. Park your car and walk over to me. No tricks, missy. I will call Paul, and Laurel won't ever forget what happens to her tonight. Do you hear me?"

"Yes, Father."

"You have five minutes."

"Yes, Father."

Nolan stamped down his rage, focusing instead on the strength of the woman he loved. He called Gideon and told him what Maggie's father said. "I don't want Maggie to be touched by this man."

"Agreed," Gideon said. "I'll tell you when I'm in position, then have Maggie start walking to him, have her yell out to him to get out of the car. I'll take it from there."

"Where are you going to take him?"

"For now I'm going to lock him in his trunk. Gotta love a Buick."

Nolan laughed. Gideon must almost be in position if he'd spotted the car.

"Drake has an idea of what to do with them after we've scooped them all up. He and some of the Midnight Delta team will be here tomorrow morning. Too bad they're going to miss all the fun," Gideon chuckled.

Nolan wanted to laugh again, but he was easing his rented SUV into Polly's parking lot and the idea of Maggie walking ten feet away from him, let alone one-hundred-and-fifty, gnawed at his guts.

He pulled into a parking spot in between two big trucks so his SUV couldn't be seen.

"Don't do anything but walk toward your dad's car. When you're within shouting distance, yell for him to get out of the car and call Paul where you can hear. If he says no, just continue to stand where you are no matter what until he gets out. Do you hear me?"

Maggie nodded.

As soon as she opened the car door, Nolan grabbed

her hand and wrenched her back toward him. He leaned over the console and ground his mouth against hers, needing to feel her, taste her, absorb her very essence. Maggie whined as she gripped the hair at the back of his head and pulled him closer. She bit his lip and when his mouth opened wider and thrust her tongue deep. They could not get enough of one another.

When she finally pulled away, there was steam on the windows and they were both panting.

"Dammit, Maggie, don't go."

"I have to. I'll do exactly what you told me. This is going to work."

"I love you."

She leaned forward and blessed him with a light kiss. "I love you too," then she rushed out of the car. As soon as she was gone, Nolan got out the driver's side door and started his way around the other cars in the parking lot. He'd parked strategically in a spot where he had a lot of cover so that he could be near Maggie as she walked toward her father.

He was two cars over when she shouted.

"I'm here, Father!"

"Come here now!"

"No, Father."

"Don't you dare backtalk me!" It was clear he was enraged. "Get your ass into the car right now."

"Not until you get out of the car and I hear you call Paul and tell him to stop hurting Laurel. Then I will do whatever you want me to."

"You never, not ever, dictate to me, little girl." The big man got out of the car and got in a wrestler's stance.

"It's your choice." Maggie's voice was calm. She turned to walk away. Nolan had never been more impressed with someone in his life.

"When I get your ass home, you will regret this. Do you hear me?"

Maggie turned back. "Does that mean you're calling Paul?"

Her father held up his cell phone and Nolan watched as he pressed a button.

"Put it on speaker phone, Father."

"You will pay for this, little girl," he yelled.

Nolan looked around. There was a family that saw what was going on, and the father was trying to hustle them away from Maggie. A man's voice came through the phone. "Father? Do you have her?"

"I do. Leave Laurel alone. We will allow Ronny to deal with her after the wedding."

"When will Margaret be back?"

"In two days at the latest. I was going to tell the VanWycks that I was in town, but I prefer to show them that we handled this within the family."

"That's a very good idea."

"Don't let her go. Keep her with you until Margaret is back home. I don't want her to try anything foolish on the drive home, do you understand me, Son?"

"I do, Father."

He hung up the phone.

"If you make me come over there and get you, you

will regret it. Sitting down on the car ride home will be agony if I hear one more bit of backtalk from you. Now heel!"

Nolan watched with satisfaction as Gideon came up behind Mr. Rhodes and used the butt of his gun to knock him unconscious. He quickly opened the back door of the Buick and slid him inside.

"I'll be back to the house in a couple of hours," Gideon said as he slid into the driver's seat. By that time Nolan was beside Maggie, but she must not have noticed since she almost jumped a foot when he put his arm around her shoulder.

"Nolan!" she cried and shoved her face into his sweater.

"You did good, Baby. You did so fucking good."

"It was too damn easy if you ask me," Ryker said for the forty-third time. Maggie curled up tighter against Nolan's side, letting him stroke her hair, her back, her feet, whatever body part he wanted to. For some reason, that little escapade in Polly's parking lot seemed to have upset him, when it was really nothing.

"The only reason it was easy is because we were dealing with the stupidest dumbfucks imaginable." Jase looked absolutely disgusted. "The good news is that not one of your pictures on the walls was damaged, Miss Trenda. Something tells me that is what's most important to you."

"You're right. Thank you for that. Alice will sure have her hands full tonight. First Arlo, now the VanWycks in her jail. I love how you were able to push them to shoot at you so it was the kind of robbery attempt where they might do some real prison time." Trenda grinned.

"Let's not get too excited yet. We still have Crazy Kyle out and about," Nolan cautioned everyone.

"I don't know, Nolan, his family means everything to him. When he finds out that they might be going to prison, I think he'll be too busy focusing on helping them and forget about me."

"Or he'll go apeshit crazier and blame it all on you," Ryker said. "Nope, do *not* let your guard down for an instant."

"Agreed," Nolan rumbled. "I couldn't have said it better myself."

"Well, we're not going any place, until Apeshit Crazy Boy is caught," Gideon said.

Jase, Ryker, and Linc all nodded, and Maggie gave a happy sigh.

"If two of you want to share a room, we have an extra room here," Trenda said. "After that, we can set the other two up at the Whispering Pines hotel."

"I'll stay here," Jase announced.

Maggie giggled, and Nolan squeezed her little toe.

"I'll pay for three rooms at the Whispering Pines," Gideon said. "Please tell me it's better than the LeeHy."

"Worse," Trenda and Nolan said at the same time.

"They're lying." Maggie grinned over at Gideon.

Maggie saw Jase wink at Trenda. Trenda rolled her eyes. Seriously, she was not having any of it.

Interesting.

It wasn't until the guys had left, and Maggie and Trenda were getting Iris and Bella ready for bed that Maggie could ask her about Jase's flirting.

"Don't you like him?" Maggie asked.

"I like him just fine. But he's not interested in knowing *me.* He hasn't asked me one personal question, he's done nothing but flirt. That's not what I want. I want somebody who's interested in me. Eventually, if it happens, I want to bring somebody into my life who can be a father to my daughter. I just don't see Jase in that role, do you?"

Sadly, Maggie didn't.

She hugged Trenda and wished her good night.

CHAPTER TWENTY-TWO

Nolan woke up in an instant. The sound of breaking glass and explosions filled the air. Within seconds a fire alarm was shrieking through the house. Maggie was beside him, and she was just as alert.

"Iris!"

"Put your shoes on," Nolan barked. Then when he realized she was just wearing one of his t-shirts, he yelled, "Pants too."

He yanked on his jeans, stepped into his boots, and turned to see how Maggie was doing. He couldn't have her go out the bedroom's balcony doors. He would bet his last dollar that he'd heard Molotov cocktails, and he didn't want her outside because it had to be Kyle. But that made no sense—wasn't it Arlo who did Molotov cocktails?

Nolan found his leather jacket, slipped into it, then grabbed his Sig Sauer pistol off the nightstand and put it into his jacket pocket.

He heard another explosion and more breaking glass. He glanced all around the room, looking for something more substantial for Maggie to wear to protect her from the flames. He shrugged out of his leather jacket, keeping the gun, then he thrust it at her.

"Put this on, and come with me." He grabbed Maggie's hand; they'd face this together.

He thought through the layout of the house. There was only one story. They were on one wing with Jase, and Trenda while Bella and Iris were on the other side of the house in the other wing in the master bedroom.

He took a step out of the bedroom.

"Jase," he roared.

"Molotov cocktails," Jase yelled back. So far no flames down this hall, but the smoke was coming fast.

"Gotta get to Trenda and the kids," Nolan yelled.

"But Apeshit is trying to flush out Maggie," Jase yelled back.

"Exactly."

"So we all go to Trenda," Jase replied.

"Hurry," Maggie yelled as she yanked on Nolan's hand. He looked down at her feet and saw that she was wearing tennis shoes. *Good.*

As soon as they were down the hall, they hit the great room and they were in hell. What had been a room that dazzled with all the incoming light from the huge windows now had broken windows with flames floor to ceiling.

Maybe he could go around the house, and go get them?

He scratched that idea. Jase needed to deal with Kyle—Nolan needed to get to Iris in the most direct manner possible, and through the great room was it.

Then Nolan felt it—rain. No, it was the sprinkler system coming on. But he looked up and wanted to scream. Barely any water was coming down at all. Something was wrong with the system. He looked into the great room again and saw some water dribbling down, causing the flames to hiss a little, but other than that, it did *nothing*!

"Jase, did you bring a gun?" Nolan yelled.

"Fuck yeah."

"Take Maggie outside. Kill that motherfucker when he tries for her."

"Save Iris," Maggie called out to him as she went with Jase.

Goddamn right I'm going to save Iris.

Nolan surveyed the great room and saw some spots where he had a chance to run with mild damage to himself—especially if he ran fast, which he fucking intended to do. He just prayed that another Molotov cocktail wouldn't come in while he was running.

He made it halfway across the great room to the large sectional sofa, when the huge light fixture came crashing down. One of the arms hit him on his shoulder and he went down on one knee.

Fuck. Fuck. Fuck.

He knew he was bleeding, but at least he wasn't on fire.

Go. Go. Go.

He made it to the hallway that led to the master bedroom. He couldn't see; so much smoke his eyes were watering too bad, so he had to close them. He just kept them closed and walked fast from memory.

"Trenda!" he yelled. "Trenda!"

He started coughing.

He tried to yell her name again but couldn't because of the coughing. He needed to get low to avoid the smoke, but he needed to get to them fast. Had Kyle done one of the bombs through their bedroom window?

He opened his eyes just a little and found the master bedroom door closed. He felt the door handle, it was cool. He opened it.

Fresh air, thank fuck.

He opened his eyes. The room was empty.

"Trenda!" he bellowed.

The bathroom door flew open.

"Nolan! We're okay. I couldn't take them outside because I knew it was Kyle, and he might—" She didn't say anything more as Bella came out of the bathroom.

"Where's Iris?" Nolan demanded to know, practically pushing past Trenda to see where his baby was. Finding her calmly holding her toes while she was strapped into her infant seat was the best picture in the world.

"Let's get you out of here." He wished like hell he had his phone and could call Jase and find out the situation outside. But he didn't have that, so he'd take it as it came. He unbuckled Iris, then picked her up as well as the little baby blanket that she was swaddled in, then turned to Trenda and Bella.

"Nolan, are we going to die?" Bella asked, tears trickling down her cheeks.

"Hell no. You have too much money to die," he grinned.

She gave him a little grin back. "You owe me a dollar."

French doors led out to a patio off the suite. The only reason that Kyle probably hadn't thrown a bomb through the window was that the blinds were so tightly shut he might not have realized they were windows. Maybe the dumbass just thought they were doors. Who cared, they had a safe way out.

"Okay, Bella, you need to be in between your mom and me. Okay? Trenda, I need you to hold Iris for me."

She gave him a stunned look.

He answered her unasked question. "I don't know what to expect out there, but I'm going to need both of my hands." Why the fuck hadn't he grabbed the Carbine up in the living room bookcase while he'd been running by?

It took him a second to unlock the doors. His arm was beginning to go numb.

Must be where the light hit me.

He started coughing again.

"Nolan, we need to call an ambulance, you're bleeding pretty badly."

"I'm fine."

He got the doors open. "Wait here."

He stepped out and found nothing. He knew that Jase had taken Maggie out on the other side of the house. Hopefully, Kyle was now a memory over there.

He turned and pulled Trenda and Bella out to the patio, then pulled them even farther until they were well away from the house. "Sit down," he said hoarsely before he coughed again. "I'm going to check on Maggie and Jase."

Trenda nodded. She was holding Iris and Bella close, a look of peace on her face.

"I've been wanting you forever, Margaret. Forever."

Maggie looked down in horror at Jase. It seemed like he was bleeding badly, but she didn't know. At least he wasn't gut-shot. She continued to stare at him, then he opened his eyes for just a moment and winked at her.

"Goddammit, look at *me*, Margaret. At *me!*"

Maggie didn't know what to do, what to say. She looked up at Kyle. He didn't look like the man she remembered. Kyle had always been dressed so well and cared about his appearance. Instead, he wasn't just disheveled, he was dirty and his clothes were in tatters, as if he had been living in the woods.

"I'm looking at you. What am I supposed to be seeing?"

"I am your husband!"

"You are not."

"I am. In the eyes of the council, in the eyes of our fathers, you belong to me."

"None of that matters to me."

There was no way she was going to tell him about Nolan. She had to calm him down. She needed to get Jase to a hospital. She needed to make sure that Iris was all right.

"I'm not taking you to Elk Bay. You'll run away again. I've found someplace else. Some place new and secure. It will just be the two of us, forever."

"You're not thinking straight. Your father will be upset."

"I am my own man," Kyle said proudly. He stepped around Jase and grabbed her arm, holding the gun to her gut. "Now you will come with me."

"Where are we going?" Maggie asked so that Jase would know.

"It's a place I found in Idaho. You'll like it."

"Where?"

Kyle shook her. "Don't ask so many questions, it's not proper for a wife to question her husband so much."

"Let her go," Nolan shouted. Maggie almost fainted, she was so relieved to know that Nolan was alive. If he was alive, that meant Iris was okay too.

Kyle twirled around, holding Maggie with him, the gun still to her stomach.

"Ah, I know you. You're the first one. I saw you at the trailer. You looked angry. I met your friend that day."

Maggie stared at Nolan. He didn't look so good. He was bleeding from his shoulder, and he looked really pale. His shoulder was sagging and he was holding his gun in his left hand, not his right hand.

"Drop the gun right now, or I'll kill you, Kyle. I mean it."

"You won't do that. Nobody ever wants to risk the damsel in distress," Kyle scoffed.

Nolan raised his gun and Maggie screamed when part of Kyle's skull splattered on her.

"Dumbass. You always go for the shot," Maggie heard Nolan say.

Nolan slumped to one knee and Maggie ran over to him. She needed a phone. They needed ambulances and fire trucks, and then Glory Hallelujah she heard a siren.

"Nolan, what's wrong with you?"

"I'm fine. What's wrong with Jase?"

"He winked at me, I think he's going to be okay. How's Iris?"

"She's with Trenda. They're all fine. I have them far from the fire in the backyard. You need to go to them."

The sirens were getting closer.

"No, I'm staying here with you."

"How touching."

Maggie turned to look at Jase. But it wasn't Jase who had said that, it was Titus Rutherford. He had his foot up on Jase's chest, and a simpler long gun trained on her.

"Move away from No-Good, Mary."

"No," she said.

Nolan stood up and gently moved her away from him. "The Molotov cocktails. Should have remembered that was how Arlo set fire to all those cabins."

"Well, you never were all that bright, now were you?" Titus stepped over Jase and moved a couple of feet forward.

Nolan laughed. "Seems to me, you're not that bright either, since you've got a gun trained on me as half the first responders of Jasper Creek are minutes away. How are you going to explain that?"

"That's the beauty, I'm not. You see, I don't care. You've ruined everything. Absolutely everything," Titus drawled as he lifted up his long gun higher. He was putting it to his eye when Nolan asked a question.

"How did I do that?"

Titus lowered it and answered, "I'll tell you how it ruined everything."

Nolan was keeping him talking like in the books!

Behind Titus, Maggie saw a movement. It was Jase! He was moving slowly. What was he doing?

"The bank's been hanging on by a thread. The only thing that was going to save it was that development, but you made sure to blow that out of the water. I'm not going to live in this town as the Rutherford who lost the bank. I refuse. But if I'm not living, neither are you."

She looked back up at Titus, his face was now mottled red. Maggie prayed he'd have a heart attack.

Her eyes shifted from Titus to Jase for just a

second. Jase had his gun in his hand. *Oh my goodness. Jase might actually be able to shoot Titus for us.*

"I should have kicked you in the head when I had the chance," Titus said.

"Yeah well, I think somebody needs to shoot you in the head," Nolan replied.

She heard a loud bang and at the same time, she watched part of Titus's head explode. She turned around and found Nolan grinning.

"Yep, you probably should have, Titus."

"That asshole sure could talk a lot," Jase choked out as his arm dropped down onto the ground.

"Thanks for the save," Nolan said as he pulled off his t-shirt, ran over to Jase, dropped down beside him, and started to apply pressure to his wound.

"Anytime, buddy. Anytime." His eyes were closed and his breathing was choppy.

"Give me my jacket," Nolan said with his hand out.

Maggie slipped it off and handed it to Nolan. He took his shirt off Jase, then folded it up so it looked like more of a bandage, then reapplied it. He took his leather jacket and covered Jase's torso and arms, being sure to keep pressure on the bandage from the outside of his jacket.

"Jase, wake up. I need you to wake up. Ambulance is almost here. Wake up."

Jase opened his eyes. "We got him?"

Nolan smiled. "You did."

Maggie turned away from the two men, then looked at the body closest to her—Kyle's. She shuddered. One of his eyeballs was hanging out of its socket. Turning away, she looked over at Titus who was twenty feet away. Part of his head was missing too; she could see some of his brain.

She tasted bile for just a moment.

How could...?

Wait, are you kidding me? she asked herself. *They both deserved it, and you should be damned glad that Nolan and Jase shot their heads off!* She started to smile.

She glanced back at Nolan and Jase. They were heroes.

"I'm going to have to learn how to shoot," she said to no one in particular.

Nolan let himself into the suite at the Whispering Pines hotel where he was staying with Maggie and Iris. Paperwork, he hated fucking paperwork, and there had been over two days' worth of it as the authorities wanted him to go through what happened with Titus and Kyle.

Sheriff Alice Mitchell had actually taken it easy on him, probably because his collarbone was broken and Jase needed surgery. Still, two days was an awful lot of time that he could have been better spent with Maggie and Iris.

Gideon had driven Maggie's father all the way back up to Elk Bay along with Linc. They gave him a couple of restroom breaks out of the trunk along the way, but according to Gideon, they were few and far between. By the time they got there, they found that some changes were already happening. It seemed that Matthew, Peter, and Brian Rhodes had become leaders of the council and were enacting changes. Brian had brought in the county sheriff to deal with Paul and Ronny for assaulting Laurel.

"You're back!" Maggie greeted him as he walked in the door. "We missed you."

Now that's what he was talking about. Maggie Rhodes—soon to be O'Rourke—was a wonder.

"I want to take you out to dinner, someplace in Gatlinburg tonight. Are you up for it?"

Maggie's look of happiness changed to one of distress. "Trenda called, she wants us to go out with Drake and his wife, and Evie and her husband tonight. Is that okay?"

"Sure. Gatlinburg can wait til another night." He bent down and kissed her. "So when am I going to see you as a blonde?"

"Trenda has something planned for me at the end of the week." Maggie smiled.

"I can't wait."

He turned to where Iris was in her infant seat on the couch. "How are you doing, Sweet Pea?"

When his little girl started gurgling and bouncing, Nolan's heart clenched. He went over and unbuckled her from her seat and gave her a long cuddle. "I missed you, little girl."

Iris grabbed at his nose. "I'll take that to mean you missed me too."

"She did, Nolan. She really did. I swear to you, when you're not here, she looks for you."

Nolan looked down at Maggie. "That's not true."

"Of course she looks for you. You're her daddy."

EPILOGUE

"Who is this Blessing woman again?" Maggie asked as they watched Iris playing on her baby blanket.

"I'm telling you, she's a mystic or something. I still can't believe how much she knew when she talked to me at the USO."

"It's too bad Scott won't be able to join y'all when you meet up in Atlanta."

"You said y'all," Nolan laughed. "I'm rubbing off on you."

Maggie waggled her eyebrows. "You sure are."

She watched as her husband got that look in his eye, the one that said she was in for a passionate night.

"Are you sure you don't want to come with me?" Nolan asked for the third or fourth time.

"I appreciate you asking, but I really need to study for my GED. I'm determined to finish that up by the end of the year."

"Do you know how proud I am of you, Mrs. O'Rourke?" Nolan said with a loving look.

"I do. I really do." And she did. Nolan said so almost every day. He had meant it when he'd said he wanted her to fly.

"Look at her go," Nolan pointed to Iris who was now crawling across the carpet. "She is so fucking fast. I've been reading a couple of baby books, and she's progressing far faster for her age."

"No!" Maggie shouted as she saw Iris pick up something from the carpet and try to put it in her mouth. She got over to her and realized she'd found a piece of carpet fuzz. She took it out of Iris's hand. "Only eat when you're in your high chair, remember?"

Iris's lower lip began to wobble.

"I really thought I got everything," Maggie moaned.

"Maggie, you vacuumed the carpet twice yesterday," Nolan chuckled.

Iris gave Maggie a disgruntled look and crawled away from her, then headed for the couch and lifted herself up. She'd been doing that for the last week. This time she did it and turned, then took two steps before landing on her diapered bottom. Instead of pouting, she had a big grin on her face—she realized she'd accomplished something big.

Maggie and Nolan both rushed over to her and landed on their knees.

"Good girl," they said simultaneously.

"Daddy is so proud," Nolan grinned.

"So is Mommy."

Iris reached out for both of her favorite people, who reached out for one another.

"I couldn't be any happier," Maggie sighed. "Thank you for making all of my dreams come true."

"You've got it all wrong, Honey. You're the miracle worker, you made everything possible in my life. I'm the luckiest man on earth."

He was so happy that he was surprising Blessing the way he was. The woman deserved it. She didn't know it, but her subtle, or not-so-subtle pushes had made a difference in all of their lives that night, and the five of them wanted to honor her.

"You're in for a treat," Blessing said as they walked up the street. "I haven't been here in ten years, but my friend and I used to come here once a month, and the steaks were wonderful."

"What happened to your friend?"

"Oh, she moved to Seattle to be closer to her son and his children."

Nolan put his hand on her lower back to usher her up the stairs to the restaurant. He had made reservations for the five of them at six forty-five so that Chris, Dylan, and Cal could get to the table first, then he told Blessing that the reservation was at seven o'clock. He should have realized she would want to be early. He prayed that his military friends were of the same mindset and were already seated as planned.

When they got to the hostess stand, he put in his name.

"The rest of your party is already seated," the hostess said.

Damn, busted.

Blessing beamed. Well, what did Nolan expect—the woman was a mystic after all. As they went down the hall toward the main restaurant, Blessing looked up at him. "Nolan, did you plan this?" she asked.

"It was a group effort," he said.

"Hmmm," was her response.

Then they got to the end of the hall, and they were in the main dining room. Nolan couldn't believe what he was seeing. His eyes were assaulted with early eighties disco colors and Vegas chandeliers. He had to blink twice before he could make out anything. It was like he had been wearing his night vision goggles and then someone had turned on the lights.

Was that a cluster of palm trees strung with Christmas lights? No wonder it was so bright; there were about one hundred mirrors refracting light everywhere. *Good God!* Was that James Dean leering down at him? Holy fuck, there *was* a disco ball! Was Al Pacino going to come out and yell, "Say hello to my little friend!" like in Scarface?

He plastered a smile on his face. "How festive." He smiled down at Blessing.

She bit her lip. "I swear to you, this is not how it was before."

Uh-oh. He had never seen her at a loss before. She truly looked upset. It was truth time.

"Blessing, we wanted a night to remember. You have given us one in spades," Nolan chuckled. "This is something we will be talking about for years to come."

Blessing's eyes started to twinkle. "You're right about that. Let's hope the food is still good."

As they wound their way around the tables, Dylan Grant, Cal Swenson, and Chris Andrews stood up.

"Hey, Blessing, you totally nailed it. This is the best restaurant ever," Cal grinned.

"I've already done a facetime with Stella. She wants to come here the next time we're in Atlanta," Chris said.

Blessing shook her head and laughed. "You boys are the best."

Nolan held out her chair and she sat down.

"Can I take your drink orders?" the hostess asked.

Nolan looked over at Blessing. She looked up at the woman. "Normally I would say a nice glass of Chardonnay, but I think tonight a Manhattan is in order."

All the men chuckled.

Nolan looked around the table and saw that everyone was drinking beer, so he put his beer order in as well.

"Before we start talking," Chris said, "I want to get

Scott in on this. He's snowed in; you know the Dakotas. I think it even snows in August," he laughed.

He pulled out his tablet and put it up on the edge of the table. Everybody said 'Hi.'

It took a while before their drinks were delivered. Everybody had time to catch each other up with their lives. Some of the stories were pretty fantastic, some were very moving. Nolan took out his phone and showed a video that soon had everybody else doing the same thing.

Finally, after what had to be a half hour, their drinks arrived.

Yep, the service matched the décor.

Not that it mattered, it was good friends that mattered.

Nolan looked over at Blessing. "I have something to say."

She looked puzzled.

He stood up and raised his beer.

"I think you know that you are a gifted woman." She bowed her head. "But what I don't know if you realize is how your caring, your compassion, and your gifts helped me to believe in myself and take the right path no matter how difficult. I will never be able to thank you enough."

The other men stood up and lifted their beers, and Nolan saw Scott Evers lifting a highball glass of what he knew to be bourbon. "To Blessing," they all said as they took a sip.

As they were all standing, Chris Andrews cleared his throat. His gaze shifted around the table to the others, including Scott. "Blessing told me that my journey would be just as important as the destination." He ducked his head and chuckled. "She also mentioned that Shakespeare said that journeys end in lovers meeting. I had no idea what she was talking about, but it turns out she was right. And I'm fuckin' glad she was. So, here's to Blessing, new friends, and journeys."

"Here, here." Everybody toasted.

"Chris, that was beautiful. And so were those pictures of Stella," Blessing said.

"Since we're still standing, I have something to say," Dylan piped up. "So often, we go through life thinking we know where we're headed. We don't, but thankfully, there are those among us that do. They appear when we begin to lose our way and guide us back to where we need to be, to the things that matter most. To Blessing and her woo-woo!" he said, raising his beer to the chuckles of the others.

"To Blessing," they all said, as she chuckled as well.

"I think it's my turn," Cal said with a grin. "Here in this fantastically horrendous, but definitely memorable establishment, I have a little story to tell you. What I didn't know back when we all first met—but found out later when I got home—was that besides what Blessing told me that day, which turned out to be completely true, was that my grandmother went to college with

Blessing's mother, Linda. They're still the best of friends. But what Blessing doesn't know..."

He looked around the table and everybody leaned in, listening intently, including Blessing.

"What she doesn't know," Cal continued, "is that my grandmother told me a little story about the day Blessing was born. Her mother was so grateful to have this beautiful, healthy baby daughter that she named her Blessing. And I have to agree it has to be a blessing that all of us met her."

His gaze zeroed in on Blessing.

"Your smile is a blessing to all of the many troops who come through the Hartsfield-Jackson International Airport USO."

He raised his beer high.

"To Blessing."

"To Blessing," everyone repeated.

Nolan saw a sheen of tears in her eyes.

"I guess that means I'm last," Scott Evers said from the tablet.

"That's what happens when you decide to live in the middle of nowhere," Chris teased.

Scott must have adjusted his camera because he was now standing up.

"To Blessing. She was my compass that pointed me to my future, leading me to my past. Her magic is priceless, her wisdom beyond compare. May you continue to direct lost souls to their future, so they find their bearings and the life they deserve."

He held up his glass of bourbon and everybody

said, "To Blessing," before they took the last sip of their drinks.

This time, there was more than a sheen of tears. Blessing had to wipe away a tear.

Nolan turned to this special woman and she reached out for a hug.

Nolan whispered quietly in her ear. "Blessing, we wouldn't be where we are without you. Thank you."

"Thank you, Nolan, for all of this," she whispered back.

"One more thing," he continued to whisper. "I have some woo-woo myself. Your day is coming, not real soon, but it's coming. And when it does, it will be magnificent."

THE LONG ROAD HOME SERIES
From the Binge Read Babes

My Heart's Home Kris Michaels
Home to Stay Maryann Jordan
Finding Home Abbie Zanders
Home Again Caitlyn O'Leary
Home Front Cat Johnson

Searching for Home Kris Michaels
Home Port Maryann Jordan
Home Base Abbie Zanders
Home Fires Cat Johnson

Defending Home Caitlyn O'Leary

Read Trenda's story, in the new Protector's of Jasper Creek Series

coming out this winter:His Wounded Heart (Book 1).

ABOUT THE AUTHOR

Caitlyn O'Leary is a USA Bestselling Author, #1 Amazon Bestselling Author and a Golden Quill Recipient from Book Viral in 2015. Hampered with a mild form of dyslexia she began memorizing books at an early age until her grandmother, the English teacher, took the time to teach her to read -- then she never stopped. She began re-writing alternate endings for her Trixie Belden books into happily-ever-afters with Trixie's platonic friend Jim. When she was home with pneumonia at twelve, she read the entire set of World Book Encyclopedias -- a little more challenging to end those happily.

Caitlyn loves writing about Alpha males with strong heroines who keep the men on their toes. There is plenty of action, suspense and humor in her books. She is never shy about tackling some of today's tough and relevant issues.

In addition to being an award-winning author of romantic suspense novels, she is a devoted aunt, an avid reader, a former corporate executive for a Fortune 100 company, and totally in love with her husband of soon-to-be twenty years.

She recently moved back home to the Pacific

Northwest from Southern California. She is so happy to see the seasons again; rain, rain and more rain. She has a large fan group on Facebook and through her e-mail list. Caitlyn is known for telling her "Caitlyn Factors", where she relates her little and big life's screw-ups. The list is long. She loves hearing and connecting with her fans on a daily basis.

Keep up with Caitlyn O'Leary:

Website: www.caitlynoleary.com
FB Reader Group: http://bit.ly/2NUZVjF
Email: caitlyn@caitlynoleary.com
Newsletter: http://bit.ly/1WIhRup

f facebook.com/Caitlyn-OLeary-Author-638771522866740

🐦 twitter.com/CaitlynOLearyNA

📷 instagram.com/caitlynoleary_author

a amazon.com/author/caitlynoleary

BB bookbub.com/authors/caitlyn-o-leary

g goodreads.com/CaitlynOLeary

P pinterest.com/caitlynoleary35

ALSO BY CAITLYN O'LEARY

PROTECTORS OF JASPER CREEK SERIES

His Wounded Heart (Book 1)

OMEGA SKY SERIES

Her Selfless Warrior (Book #1)

Her Unflinching Warrior (Book #2)

Her Wild Warrior (Book #3)

Her Fearless Warrior (Book 4)

NIGHT STORM SERIES

Her Ruthless Protector (Book #1)

Her Tempting Protector (Book #2)

Her Chosen Protector (Book #3)

Her Intense Protector (Book #4)

Her Sensual Protector (Book #5)

Her Faithful Protector (Book #6)

Her Noble Protector (Book #7)

Her Righteous Protector (Book #8)

NIGHT STORM LEGACY SERIES

Lawson & Jill (Book 1)

The Midnight Delta Series

Her Vigilant Seal (Book #1)

Her Loyal Seal (Book #2)

Her Adoring Seal (Book #3)

Sealed with a Kiss (Book #4)

Her Daring Seal (Book #5)

Her Fierce Seal (Book #6)

A Seals Vigilant Heart (Book #7)

Her Dominant Seal (Book #8)

Her Relentless Seal (Book #9)

Her Treasured Seal (Book #10)

Her Unbroken Seal (Book #11)

Black Dawn Series

Her Steadfast Hero (Book #1)

Her Devoted Hero (Book #2)

Her Passionate Hero (Book #3)

Her Wicked Hero (Book #4)

Her Guarded Hero (Book #5)

Her Captivated Hero (Book #6)

Her Honorable Hero (Book #7)

Her Loving Hero (Book #8)

The Found Series

Revealed (Book #1)

Forsaken (Book #2)

Healed (Book #3)

SHADOWS ALLIANCE SERIES

Declan